Becky Meets Her Match

Becky Meets Her Match

Linda Byler

Good Books

New York, New York

BECKY MEETS HER MATCH

Copyright © 2016 by Linda Byler
All rights reserved. No part of this book may be reproduced in any manner without the express written consent of the publisher, except in the case of brief excerpts in critical reviews or articles. All inquiries should be addressed to Good Books, 307 West 36th Street, 11th Floor, New York, NY 10018.

Good Books books may be purchased in bulk at special discounts for sales promotion, corporate gifts, fund-raising, or educational purposes. Special editions can also be created to specifications. For details, contact the Special Sales Department, Good Books, 307 West 36th Street, 11th Floor, New York, NY 10018 or info@skyhorsepublishing.com.

Good Books is an imprint of Skyhorse Publishing, Inc.®, a Delaware corporation.

Visit our website at www.goodbooks.com.

10 9 8 7 6 5 4 3 2

Library of Congress Cataloging-in-Publication Data is available on file.

ISBN: 978-1-68099-178-9
eBook ISBN: 978-1-68099-179-6

Cover design by Koechel Peterson & Associates, Inc., Minneapolis, Minnesota

Printed in the United States of America

Table of Contents

CHAPTER 1

SHE HAD ALWAYS BEEN BIGGER, EVEN AS A BABY. She arrived on a cold November morning, round-faced and squalling, her arms already dimpled, the little rings above her feet announcing strength. She was a beautiful baby, the second daughter to be born into the Enos Esh family.

After four boys, first daughter Nancy had brought jubilation to Enos and Sadie. She had been long awaited. Then a few years later came daughter number two. Rebecca, they named her. Rebecca Lynn.

The four boys lined up by their mother's bed in the light of the propane lamp that hissed quietly above their heads. Peering at the baby's dimpled round face, they nodded politely, smiled shyly, then left to confer among themselves, away from the serious faces of their parents, who had hearing far above average.

"She's fat," said Abner.

"Red." Junior nodded.

"Shaped like a tomato," Aaron commented, a touch of sorrow and disappointment flavoring his words.

"One girl was plenty," Jake said, mourning her arrival.

No one knew exactly where or how she arrived, but the boys figured the midwife's bag was plenty big enough. The baby seemed to have come dressed in a cuddly pink blanket and sleeper.

To be born the second daughter, with four boys before her, placed Becky in the dubious position of being watched.

Monitored, supervised, observed, kept track of, and tattled on, her every misdeed recorded accurately by the queenly Nancy and her consorts, Aaron, Abner, Junior, and Jake, Becky grew into babyhood, then toddlerdom. She rolled around the kitchen on her little legs, tightly packed and sturdy like sausages.

She was cute, all right, with eyes like a trout pool, green and flecked with gold, amber, and undisturbed. Her hair was blonde with darker streaks, an unusual combination, and one no hairdresser could have imitated. Her small pug nose was like a button, her mouth wide, often stretched by her good humor. To Becky, life was funny and full of things that made her laugh, which she did often and with her whole self.

Nancy kept her in line, a mother hen who clucked and herded and denied her the freedom of making her own choices, always shored up by four pairs of disapproving eyes—Abner's, Aaron's, Junior's, and Jake's.

Becky was a whiz in school. She flew through the Spunky Arithmetic workbooks, getting 100 percent on almost every page, where she always wrote her name neatly on top—Rebecca Lynn Esh. She read the Laura Ingalls Wilder books in second grade. And she raised an eager, flapping hand for every question the teacher asked. Even then, the buttons down the back of her dress were straining to keep the fabric around her sturdy little body, the black pinafore-type apron tight beneath her arms.

Nancy, in fourth grade, thin, proper, and un-impressed, felt a blush of shame. She blinked self-consciously and lowered her head behind her spelling book. It was just that Becky was so terribly enthused, so sure of herself, and so wide. She was also short, with her too-tight dress and an appetite like a steam-roller.

Becky inhaled her baggie of potato chips, trailing embarrassing crumbs that fell from her mouth when she laughed, all recess long.

And so Becky grew up under Nancy's well meaning tutelage. She listened seriously when Nancy tried to steer her on the straight and narrow, especially when it came to her sandwiches, which were numerous, highly anticipated, and appreciated. She ate with so much gusto and gratitude as the mayonnaise oozed into white puddles on her varnished desktop. That in no way curbed her joy of food.

Food was the bliss in her lunchbox, bringing her gaiety between slices of salty ham and pleasure in the crunch of pretzels, coupled perfectly with creamy cheese chunks.

She always unwrapped a butterscotch krimpet, that Tastykake wonder, with utmost care, so as not to disturb the perfection of its rich, smooth icing. Food was a wonder, the source of endless refreshment, the axis of her world.

When Nancy was in eighth grade, the last of her school years, she was already blossoming into young womanhood, conscious of her small waist, the length of her skirt, the make of her sleeves. Sixth-grader Becky was allowed to play baseball with the upper grades that year. Nancy suffered the humiliation of her rotund sister's noisy exuberance, her uninhibited yells when her team scored a victory, the pumping of her legs beneath too-tight skirts as she lumbered to second base. Becky's pretty, round face was the color of a pickled red beet, her bun coming loose from its hairpins, with unattractive *strubles* of hair sticking out from behind her red ears.

Oh, she could hit. She could bat that softball across the fence like the boys, the eighth-grade boys. She could catch and throw like a boy, too. She was often asked to be the pitcher, drawing back her arm and letting loose a blistering throw that resulted in wails of disapproval from the opposing team.

But little by little, Nancy's words of rebuke ate away at Becky's abundance of faith in herself. Like waves washing over rocks every hour of the day and night, the thrust of Nancy's words corroded her confidence, small annoyances that lodged in her mind.

First, it was the statement that *no one* needed, actually *needed,* two sandwiches in their lunchbox. Then it was a comment about the way she ran. "Don't put your knees up so far. You put your head down and your knees up. It just looks so . . ."

Becky fired back, explaining why she ran as she did. But Nancy's words stuck, sometimes retreating and hiding in the recesses of her mind, then coming out to taunt her like mocking ghosts when she lay in bed, snuggled under the fleece comforter on a cold January night.

By the time Becky reached eighth grade and Nancy had attended vocational class, graduated, turned sixteen, and begun her years of *rumschpringa,* most of Becky's self-worth had become a faded memory. She lived in the shadow of her beautiful, slim, older sister, who regaled her adoring Mam with stories of her popularity, of the guys who spoke to her, of the gaggle of girls she hung out with, the dresses they bought and sewed, the shoes they discussed.

The boys, those four older brothers, were Becky's buddies, but they were boys, living in their own *rumschpringa* world. Abner was already thinking of marrying a girl from New York, who was shaped like a yardstick and ate only carrots and applesauce, as far as Becky could tell.

Sometimes, Mam encouraged her to lose weight by buying cases of Diet Pepsi and low-calorie lunch meat, like Oscar Mayer's turkey breast that wasn't smoked or salty. But you couldn't taste much difference between it and the package it came in.

And sometimes, Becky took it upon herself to lose weight, the bottom of her Rubbermaid Lunchmate rattling loosely with one small Fuji apple, a bag of carrot sticks, and ranch dressing. On those days, all the color went out of Becky's world, the gray mist of deprivation settled over everything, the schoolhouse and playground were places without joy.

She often reckoned that if they didn't live on a farm and she didn't have quite so many barn chores, her appetite would surely lessen.

If she had only an apple and carrots in her lunchbox, how was a girl expected to keep up her strength?

So she sneaked cupcakes or peanut butter crackers or Oreos out of the pantry. When Mam and Nancy weren't looking, she sat behind the henhouse and stuffed every morsel into her mouth, replenishing body and spirit.

The farm required lots of hard work, that was the thing. With her bandana stretched tightly across her forehead, over her ears, and under her bun of pinned up hair, she felt ready for anything. She felt like a biker on his Harley-Davidson, leaning back in the seat and roaring down a long Texas road.

She smiled to herself at that thought, leaned her head against a cow's flank, and laughed outright, her spirit buoyed by a handful of molasses cookies. When she was younger, she would have told that funny thought to the boys or Nancy, but no longer. Nancy wouldn't think it was funny, and Abner would scold her. He had become pretty close to the Bible's description of the scribes and Pharisees since he joined the church. Aaron would make fun of her, and Junior and Jake would try not to laugh, although they often did, gasping for breath once she was out of sight.

Becky's view of the world and its inhabitants was just plain amusing. Her brain worked differently than most people's. How she came up with some of the things she said was far beyond what her long-suffering parents could imagine, except Dat said his brother Ike came close. So Mam always figured Becky's humor and quick wit ran in her genes from the Esh side, but where in the world was there such an overweight young person on either side?

There wasn't. The Eshes were all lean and rangy, hardworking muscular men and women, who ate food to keep their strength up, without any interest in cooking fancy dishes or high-calorie desserts. The women cooked meat and potatoes, dumped a bag of frozen corn or peas, perhaps lima beans, into a sauce-pot with salt and butter, added a dish of applesauce or brown butter noodles to the table, and that was their supper.

Neither were the Fishers overweight on Mam's side. There were a few chunky women, after giving birth to ten or more children, but not like Becky. So Mam clucked to herself, becoming slightly more anxious as the months went by in quick succession.

Surely, she'd lose weight at fifteen, after she finished vocational class. She would.

Becky breezed through vocational class, keeping her diary where she enumerated her farm chores and detailed her education for becoming an Amish housewife. She graduated, framed the certificate, and hung it on her bedroom wall, but she never lost a pound. Her continued interest in all things edible was a source of irritation to her older sister and a secret concern of Mam's, although they both did a commendable job of hiding this.

Sometimes, when Becky slurped rapid spoonfuls of Cinnamon Life, her favorite cereal, Nancy would clear her throat and make some snide remark, which seemed not to penetrate her sister's consciousness at all. But Becky was wondering how Nancy could presume to know how hungry she was. After all, Nancy didn't help with the milking. She had a job. A job that started with a capital J, as if that was a title. It was an important thing, Nancy's job. It supplied Mam with her week's supply of grocery money, or money for the greenhouse or Walmart or Target or the fabric store, whatever.

Nancy made a lot of money, but she was only allowed to keep one-fourth of it. The rest was supposedly Mam's. This made no sense to Becky, since most of that money went right back to Nancy. Mam spent it on quilts and hope chest stuff and Tupperware and Princess House things for Nancy, who wasn't even dating. "Not that she didn't have the opportunity," Mam would always add. Well, she should be dating, Becky thought, with all that Tupperware melting in the attic.

And they sewed. They sewed endlessly. Blue dresses and green dresses and red and purple and pink. Every event needed a new dress. Becky sat on the recliner with a bag of Starburst Jellybeans and listened to the steady humming of the sewing machine. She wondered when her turn would come. Likely Mam wouldn't sew for her, as big as she was.

When Becky's sixteenth birthday loomed a few months away, she was still short and as round as a barrel. She weighed herself in secret, but told no one, not even her closest friend, that she weighed only a sliver away from two hundred pounds.

She didn't feel that big. She never had and never would. Inside, she felt just like the thin girls. In her own eyes, she looked like them. Only the scales revealed her sincere love of food.

When Mam approached her about starting to sew dresses for her sixteenth birthday, Becky shrugged, said something that showed she didn't care at all, not one smidgen, and went right on polishing off a bag of Uncle Henry's hard pretzels, her favorite.

Then there was the question of someone hiring Becky. She needed a job. Having been content to help on the farm, doing the morning and evening milking with her father, feeding calves and the Rhode Island Reds in the henhouse, driving a team of brown mules hitched to the harrow or the baler, helping her mother in the garden, then canning, preserving, and freezing the large amounts of vegetables they put up every year, Becky never imagined having an actual job. But it became a real requirement now.

With her sixteenth birthday just over the horizon, an unknown and very scary event she could not avoid, she figured she may as well face this thing head on and get a job since Mam kept hinting around.

There was the local Amish bulk-food store, the greenhouse in Waverly, the households in town who were always looking for cleaning help. There were the two dry-goods stores and a few nearby restaurants. She could babysit other people's children, but the pay was low, the children weren't always obedient, and the mothers could be very picky. She was ready to cross that possibility off the list.

She mulled over her predicament as she peeled potatoes one evening in September. The sky was streaked with red and purple, turning the brown grasses that looked old and worn out into a beautiful sea of deep indigo, the leaves on the trees a richer shade of green.

Nancy came to stand beside her, with that sniff which meant she was about to make an important announcement. Becky kept on peeling potatoes stiffly.

"So little sister," Nancy drawled, the condescension oozing from her words like cornstarch pudding in a Boston cream pie.

Becky chose to direct her utmost attention to peeling the potatoes.

"So," Nancy began again, drawing a deep breath. "So, you'll be with the youth before you know it, Becky, which means you'll need new dresses. That's exciting for you, right?"

"I guess so."

"Well, I don't want to hurt your feelings in any way, but I told Mam I would try and talk to you. You see, Becky, it would be much easier to make your dresses and buy shoes if you lost weight. I thought maybe you'd be willing to go on this Weight Watchers program. I have all the books you'll need. You don't count calories; you just go by a points system."

Becky threw the last cut potato into the pot of cold water, set the kettle on the gas range, and flipped the burner knob. She turned to look squarely at her sister, keeping her face without expression, as bland and flat as a vanilla cookie.

"I mean, you know Becky, don't be hurt by what I'm saying."

Becky lifted her shoulders and let them fall. "I'm not."

"Good. All I'm saying is it's just too bad you aren't a bit, uh, thinner. You're so pretty and have a nice personality, and you could easily have a boyfriend if you weren't . . ."

"So fat," Becky finished.

"That's not a nice way to say it. I don't mean it like that."

"It's okay, Nancy. Really."

"So you'll try?"

Becky scraped the potato peelings into the garbage and nodded, promising her sister that, yes, she'd look at the Weight Watchers plan.

Later, she caught Nancy and her mother casting quick, nervous glances toward her as they held a whispered conversation in the kitchen.

Becky showered, brushed her teeth, and went to bed early. The evening was chilly, and she was tired from a day of driving the hay wagon, picking up the last of the fourth cutting of alfalfa. The bales had been wet and cold and heavy.

She turned up the battery lamp by her bed, grabbed her book, and tried to read, but the words blurred across the page as if they were swimming. She put the book down, swiped fiercely at her eyes, and switched off her lamp. She lay flat, crossed her hands

across her soft, round stomach, and thought very seriously about her life so far, what she expected in the
future, and what was most important.

So would the whole world change because she
reached her sixteenth year? No, it would not. She
would still be Becky Esh. Short and round, and yes,
fat. Would that be so awful? Would her friends desert
her and God dislike her for being fat? No.

So who would judge her? Only people like Nancy
and Mam, who were ashamed of her. Well, let them
be ashamed. That would be just fine.

No one was going to make her feel small or take
away her confidence. She would not let them.

Becky had no intention of even looking at that stupid weight-loss literature. If Nancy thought for one
minute that she was going to weigh tiny portions
of food on a scale, or check how many points were
in a whoopie pie or a banana, well, she could think
again.

I am just me, no more, no less. I was born to love
food, and if I am a larger size than some girls, who
cares? I am me. Rebecca Lynn Esh. I have the whole

future ahead of me, and I will not cringe and be ashamed of who I am. If people don't like me, well, that's just tough.

She cried a bit then. She wasn't aware of it really. She just felt two tears slide down the side of her face, tickling her cheeks. She felt sad and elated, happy to have arrived at this wisdom, this knowledge of her own self-worth.

No one can take away this feeling of inner confidence when they don't know it's there, now can they? Not even Mam or Nancy. So I won't make a fuss. I'll just *act* as if I'm reading the booklet.

She sighed, sniffed, rolled over once, and fell into a deep, restful sleep.

As the autumn days went by, the Wisconsin landscape changed from the brown and dull greens of a summer without sufficient rainfall, to a panorama of golds and brilliant reds and oranges. Frost was in the morning air, nipping Becky's nose. She stumbled to the barn, wiping the sleep from her bleary eyes. She had overslept and developed a sore throat, so Jake took her turn at the milking.

Upon reaching the milk house, Becky threw some calf starter into a plastic bottle, added water, and shook it, then started another bottle. They had a whole line of white calf hutches behind the barn, filled with the knobby-kneed, doe-eyed little creatures she loved. She knew each one by the markings on their coats and the names she gave them. Ivy, Mollie, Sadie, Gina, Lily, and Bena.

The milk house door swung open, and her father came through, his old straw hat torn and bent, his heavy blue shirt wrinkled but clean, his eyes twinkling at her behind his glasses. His beard was long and thick and already tinged with gray along the sides.

"Well, there you are, Becky," he said, a wide smile creasing his kindly features.

Becky grunted and kept mixing calf starter.

"Didn't sleep so good, did you?"

Becky shook her head.

"You're getting nervous with that long awaited sixteenth birthday rolling around, huh?"

Becky shrugged her shoulders.

"Oh, come on. You know you're looking forward to your *rumschpringa.*"

"Not according to Mam and Nancy."

Dat's eyes narrowed. He set down the bucket he was carrying, leaned against the bulk tank, and crossed his arms. "What do you mean by that?"

"I'm too fat."

For a long moment Dat said nothing. Becky knew he was a man of few words, especially at emotional times, so she picked up the bottles of calf starter, preparing to lean against the milk house door to open it, when he spoke.

"Becky, don't let them change you. Believe me, you will make some lucky guy a wonderful wife."

If Dat had been an English father, he would have hugged Becky, holding her close for the comfort and love a hug provided. As it was, his words wrapped themselves around her like arms, and she smiled with her eyes, then quickly exited.

The morning took on a rosy hue. Diamonds sparkled in the dew-topped grass; the air was magical and filled with promise. The birds sang their liquid notes; the mockingbird put on his own personal show from the yellow sugar maple. Dat's words filled Becky's world with color. Her steps became sure and firm as she held her head high on this wonderful day. She nuzzled the top of Ivy's head with her face, breathing in her little cow smell.

At the breakfast table, she helped herself to two fried eggs, three sausages, and a hefty slice of home-made toast, without sparing the butter and strawberry jam. She also polished off two pancakes, topped with more butter and syrup.

Nancy was absent, having gone to market early. She worked at a bakery in a farmer's market in the local town of Concord, so her driver picked her up at 4:30 in the morning. Abner and Aaron were off to their construction jobs, leaving only Junior, Jake, and Becky at the morning table.

Mam drank her coffee, throwing worried glances in her hungry daughter's direction, sighed with her mouth compressed, but said nothing.

Dat discussed the day's work with the boys and asked Becky if she was available to drive the horses to finish up the haying. "Supposed to rain tomorrow," he said.

"Well, then, we'll plan on going to the dry-goods store, Becky. We need to sew for you," Mam interjected.

Becky looked up from her plate, waiting for Mam's smile that always appeared for Nancy, along with eagerness and poorly concealed pride. But the smile was absent and never showed up; only raised eyebrows and a concerned look filled Mam's worried eyes.

Becky said nothing.

"Big times coming for little sister," Jake grinned.

Mam did smile, then, at Jake. "I'm sure you and Junior will take good care of her."

"Of course."

Which was comforting to a degree. Becky knew she would never have to worry about a ride to the supper crowd or the hymn-singings on Sundays. But on Saturday nights her brothers went to functions with their friends—volleyball games or ping-pong tournaments—so she'd likely not be wanted then.

Mam sipped her coffee as the boys headed to the barn.

"Becky needs a job now," she announced.

Dat looked at his wife, patience written on his face. "You think?"

"Why, Enos, of course."

"What's wrong with letting her stay right here on the farm? She's such a good hired hand."

"What about her dresses? And coats? Shoes and a bedroom suite, paint and curtains. Enos, it costs to have a daughter turn sixteen."

"I'll pay her a weekly wage."

Mam swallowed the huffy retort that rose to her lips. Becky could tell by the way she began to speak, then closed her mouth and looked pained, as if not saying the words she wanted to was like having a ping-pong ball stuck in her throat.

"Whatever you think best, Enos," Mam said, but the pained expression stayed, meaning the ping-pong ball in her throat had likely settled in her stomach now.

"Why sure, Becky. How about thirty dollars a day? That's 150 dollars a week. That will buy you anything you need."

That was an awful lot of money. "I don't need that much," she said.

"You will, Becky. If you pay for your new things," Mam said, a touch of weariness in her disappointed face.

So, this was the picture. She was turning sixteen, she would stay at home on the farm, collect her wages, buy her own dresses and shoes, and still be able to save some. That was a good deal. She sat up straighter, looked around the table, and said quite cheerily, "Well, sounds like a deal. I'll be happy to stay here on the farm. I dreaded going out and getting a job."

"You'd make a lot more money," Mam said.

"I'd also have a lot less fun. I love the farmwork, Mam. I'm happy here with the barn, the animals, the fieldwork."

Dat beamed.

Mam smiled at her, with the ping-pong ball lodged firmly in her throat again, Becky imagined.

CHAPTER 2

THE WISCONSIN LANDSCAPE WAS FLAT AND mountainless, with Amish homesteads dotted across the well managed squares of farmland, separated by trees growing in fencerows, or plots of trees that were big enough to be called a woods. Streams and ponds collected the rainwater, and underground spring water gurgled and shimmered in the crisp fall air, hosting the crappie, bluegill, and trout that swam in their waters.

The fields rang with the sound of horses and wagons, choppers and balers, as the busy farmers hurried to get in the last of the fall crops. Winters were long and cold and harsh as far north as this land lay, so the people knew to be prepared. The barns, silos, and long white mounds of plastic bulged with corn silage, hay and corn fodder, straw, and shavings.

When cold hung across the land in the fall of the year, it was the signal to become serious, to get ready for winter's frigid blast of arctic air that would come roaring in, filled with ice and snow and numbing cold. Hydrants were wrapped with insulation, straw bales banked on the north side of heifer barns, and blades were attached to horse-drawn equipment so they could function as snowplows of a sort. At least they worked well enough to remove snow from around the buildings and out the drive so the milk truck could make its entrance and exit.

Enos Esh's farm was located at the northern end of the settlement. The large red barn had been enlarged with a new dairy barn jutting out the front; its new steel siding was also red, to match the paint on the old structure. The house was white, built in the forties, a plain, square, cracker box of a house with a narrow porch along the front and a redwood-stained patio on the back. Shrubs and trees dotted along the side of the house, a kind of adornment to ease the severity of the house itself.

They had remodeled some. Enos thought Sadie should have new kitchen cabinets and linoleum, which had made a world of difference to his wife. He had persuaded her to move to Wisconsin from her life of security and ease in Lancaster County.

She had left a brand new house built of stone and beige siding, landscaped to perfection, with the barn matching the house. A fancy place, they had. Or so some thought, shaking their heads and saying *Enos sei Sadie* always got what she wanted. But then, Enos had a good business, installing seamless gutters the way he did.

All that changed when Enos decided that each of his four boys needed a farm, and there was no way he could pay a million dollars for Lancaster's rich, productive farmland.

Sadie balked. "Why Wisconsin? Enos, *siss net chide*. Why not Perry County or Dauphin County or even Sugar Valley, where you can hire a driver and in a few hours be home with the *freundshaft*?" she asked.

But Enos had his heart set on Wisconsin. His uncle Abe lived there, and Sadie's sister Ruth. (Here Sadie reminded Enos of the awful homesickness Ruth had endured, brave soul.)

In the end, they made the trip out there several times. Sadie felt the need for daily prayer, eventually feeling the will of God slowly settling around her shoulders as she searched the Scripture for direction.

She couldn't get away from it. "Whither thou goest, I will go," as Ruth said in the Bible. Abraham's wife, Sarah—now what if she had thrown a tantrum and refused to go when God called her husband to go forth? And "Wives, submit to your husbands," in the New Testament. Over and over, there it was, in black and white.

For a long time, she coasted along in the gray area of her own making, thinking that if Enos loved her the way a man should love his wife, he'd give up his will and stay in Lancaster.

And yet she knew Enos was right. Their four rowdy boys each needed a farm.

And so they went. They packed their belongings in two tractor trailers, bade their families staunch if tearful farewells, and moved a thousand miles away to a run-down, old farm that held all the charm of a broken toenail.

Becky was born in Wisconsin, the only one of their children. Sometimes Sadie thought, grimly, perhaps the Wisconsin air and water had something to do with her being so large. Although she knew better. Somewhere, somehow, generations back, there was likely a gene that traveled along in the Esh family or hers, which caused someone to have an inherited love of all things edible, especially breads and pastries.

And so Sadie gathered her courage and gave herself up to having a daughter who would be part of that world of teenagers who weighed, she guessed, close to two hundred pounds. She bought the fabric, taught an unwilling and restrained Becky to sew, then finally gave up and chased her out of the house to help her father. Sadie sat down and sewed a whole row of short, wide dresses.

She held them up, shook her head, then pressed them. Next, she made large capes and enormous black aprons that she wrapped around herself when no one was looking, marveling at the size of her daughter, the absolute largeness.

She confided in her sister Ruth, who had five daughters of her own, every one lean, rangy, hardworking, and blessed with a metabolism that disposed easily of any calories they consumed. Nor did they have interest in doughnuts and homemade pizza and candy bars.

"Oh, but she's so pretty," Ruth said. "She has the most beautiful face, her hair is combed so neat, her covering so clean and perfect. Lydia can hardly wait till Becky goes along to the youth crowds." Inwardly, Sadie cringed, thinking of Ruth's Lydia being Becky's best friend. Inseparable, they were, at that. Lydia was tall and willowy, athletic, one of the top volleyball players. Would Becky even be able to play?

Well, enough of this. Mentally, she shook herself. Too much emphasis was put on looks, according to the ways of the world. How was she any different, struggling along like this? She would pray to God and have faith that Becky would be accepted, perhaps not by the most popular ones, but at least enough to make her own way.

Ach, there was no denying it, Amish or English or Mennonite or anything, even Chinese or African American, we all—every one of us—care about our daughters when they grow up to be a marriageable age. We just do.

She thought of herself and her friend Dorcas Rissler and of Stacy who took her for groceries in her minivan. All of them together, were they so much different when it came right down to it? The concern for daughters was universal.

And there was Nancy who could have any eligible young man. Surely this would be hard for Becky as the years went by and no one asked her to be his girlfriend. So she went home and made five pumpkin pies, mixed up a batch of chocolate chip cookies, and made macaroni salad and fried chicken for supper.

They painted Becky's room white.

"Why white?" Nancy sniffed.

Becky stopped her roller long enough to glare at her and said she liked the simplicity of it. "Cool and restful," and she could decorate any way she wanted if her new bedroom furniture was black.

"Are you actually getting black furniture?" Nancy asked, incredulous.

Becky faced her sister, hands on her hips, her triangled bandana crooked on her head, paint splattered all over her navy blue dress that was straining at every seam.

"I sure am. This is my room, Nance, my colors, my choice, and if you don't like it, well, then, you don't have to. I do."

Nancy's eyes widened, and she said nothing more, taken by surprise. After a few minutes, she asked, "What color will your curtains be?"

"I really don't know. I'll have to see after my furniture is delivered."

Mam plied her trimming brush, looked from one daughter to another, and felt sorry for Nancy's lack of wit. But Nancy always knew things—what color was popular, how to decorate, where to buy things that made a young girl's room attractive.

"I might not have curtains," Becky said, breezily.

"You have to."

"No, I don't."

"What would you do without curtains?"

"Look out the windows."

Nancy smiled, then grinned widely. "And everyone would be able to look in."

"Not upstairs."

Nancy sat on the bed watching Becky move the roller expertly down the walls, then back up, over and over, doing an excellent job. The walls looked fresh and clean, but so very, very white.

Becky's arms were spilling out of the too tight and too short sleeves, her elbows dimpled with excess flesh. Nancy tried to be kind, but tact was not her best talent, so she blurted, "Your arms look twice as big when the sleeves are too tight."

Becky went right on rolling the white paint.

"Really? Well, now ain't that somepin'?"

Nancy laughed along with Becky, but her smile didn't last very long, dwindling down to a lopsided chuckle that contained a wee bit of dashed pride. It was almost as if Becky had turned the remark about fat arms on her sister. Nancy wasn't used to feeling self-conscious, but somehow, by some trick of Becky's, she did.

Nancy wandered away into her own room that was painted a dusty teal color and furnished with an oak bedroom suite and curtains to match the blue-green of her comforter. She had always loved her room and still did, as she shook off the feeling of being outdone.

What was coming over Becky? She seemed to have some secret ingredient firmly in hand as she approached her sixteenth birthday like a barge on a river, every engine put to its full capacity, churning big and steady and sure of herself, her eyes wide open, enjoying all of it. Never mind her size!

Oh, she must never confide in Becky what she herself had gone through. Not only was she intimidated by her cousins and feeling as if Mam didn't make her dresses right, her hair was thin on one side, leaving a bald spot when she wet it or rolled it higher, the way some girls did when they approached *rumschpringa*.

Her coverings seemed dowdy compared to some of the girls' in her group, and it never failed, before a weekend rolled around, that she developed either a rash of pimples, a nervous tic in her eye, or a greasy nose.

Mam had been a tremendous boost to her flagging sense of self-worth, praising her ability to comb her hair and the way she walked in her new shoes. She could tell Mam was as excited as she was the first time the neighbor boy, Leon Miller, came to pick her up. To this day, Mam's understanding, and the esteem in which she held her oldest daughter, boosted Nancy to a pinnacle where she could accept herself.

So how would Mam and Becky manage together? For starters, what had become of the Weight Watchers program? Actually, the glossy booklet was kept in the top drawer of Becky's nightstand, unused and forgotten. Every once in a while, when Becky would feel too full of Mam's meat loaf or coconut pie, she would reach under her pile of books and retrieve it. She'd flip the pages and read the calorie content of this or that, never seriously considering that she could apply one ounce of brain power to calculate her day's food intake.

What a waste of time and energy, really, Becky thought. Especially if you were a farm girl. All that heavy lifting, sweeping, switching milkers, jostling around on various pieces of farm equipment, even hanging on to the reins of rowdy horses—well, Weight Watchers was not started with Amish farm girls in mind.

Becky's birthday, November 22, was cold and blustery. Raw air crept underneath gloves and coats, tugged at head scarves and hats, and sent folks scuttling from house to barn, heads bent, hands placed firmly on the tops of battered old straw hats.

Out on the south ten acres, the rusty squeaking of the old disc harrow stayed in harmony with Becky's voice, her scarf ends whipping in the wind, dust and bits of dead, brown corn fodder whacking her face. She was singing at the top of her voice, belting out some old song from school. Her cheeks were red with the cold, her hands clutching the flat leather reins as she kept the horses in line.

Today was the day. She was surprised to feel unexpected tears well up, run over, and trail down her cheeks. Before the wind dried them, a river of tears followed. She stopped singing, allowing her mouth and eyes to scrunch up as she cried in earnest.

The thing was, this whole *rumschpringa* business made her sad. She did not want to be sixteen years old. She wanted to be thirteen or fourteen, sleep at Lydia's house in her huge flannel pajamas, and play Yahtzee without one care in the whole world.

Why was it required to start running around? Oh, she knew better than to dwell on the question. She had asked Mam and Nancy, and they said she didn't have to start at sixteen; she could stay home. But both their eyebrows were raised in that anxious way, like umbrellas over eyes wet with pity.

They felt sorry for her, large and unprepared, a loaf of bread left on the counter to rise too long.

She was fat, that was the thing, so why add the oddity of staying home to that dubious trait. Being heavier than the "normal" girls was like growing a pair of horns on each side of her head, and this she told Mam, who protested wildly, saying "Oh no," over and over, and lifting her hands to ward off Becky's words. But in the end, when all the artificial exclaiming stopped, she met Mam's eyes deeply, and they both knew the truth.

Becky cried, gasping and gulping, hiccupping and sobbing. She cried for her carefree years, for having to grow up, for the futility of wishing she wasn't who she was. Then she reached into her coat pocket, blew her nose, wiped it, dried her eyes, and stopped. It was here, now, her sixteenth birthday, and she would make something of it.

She dressed carefully in her newly redecorated room. (The curtains were gray and white.) She arranged all the pillows on her bed, adjusted the new comforter just right, then went downstairs to meet her first arrival, Lydia, her best friend.

Mam was mixing the spinach and bacon dip; Nancy was arranging crackers on a tray. The large birthday cake had been delivered from the local Weis Market and was hidden away in the pantry. There would be around fifty *youngie*, the young folks from ages sixteen to twenty-five, or older.

Becky knew most of the girls, a few as friends, but most as acquaintances. The only boys she knew were Jake's friends, Ray and Ivan, and her cousins, so naturally she was extremely nervous.

Lydia accompanied her upstairs, shrieking at Becky's "plum-down crazy" room, which delighted Becky and bolstered her courage, at least for a few moments. When the other girls, or most of them, made a fuss about her room, Becky laughed aloud, completely surprised that her taste in decorating would make such an impact.

But when the time came to gather in the kitchen, when the cake was brought out, the candles lit, and everyone sang "Happy Birthday," she would have loved to crawl under the table, pull the tablecloth around herself, and stay there.

But she smiled, her even white teeth flashing, her eyes lit up by the small flames of the sixteen candles. She opened her gifts—yards of fabric to make into dresses, pretty vases and lamp shades, journals and picture frames. Lots of cards held twenty-dollar bills or ten-dollar ones, all of them with handwritten con-gratulations and best wishes, or "May the Lord bless your sixteenth year." Some of them contained poems and spiritual verses of guidance for teenagers.

Because of the cold, they played games in the shop, lit by gas lanterns and Makita battery lamps. Ping-pong was going in one corner, ringed by a group of cheering boys; shuffleboard in another. A few card games had started along the opposite wall.

Lydia stood with Becky, her support for the eve-ning, a head taller and about half as wide. When two boys asked them to play a game of Rook, Lydia's face lit up, but she checked to see if it was okay with Becky.

Aaron Fisher's Elam was the one boy. Tall, brown-haired, and brown-eyed, with a spattering of freckles dotting his nose, he had a quick smile with one crooked tooth. Becky instantly liked him.

The other one was even taller and thin as a rail, with long arms and legs. His back stooped a bit; his hair was like straw in both color and texture. Becky couldn't tell what color his eyes were. They looked half-closed and small to begin with.

His name was Daniel, but everyone called him Jack. "For what? Why that name?" Becky wanted to know.

Daniel looked at Becky, never changed his expression, and said dryly, "They say I look like my dog."

For some reason, that tickled Becky, and before she could stop it, her laugh—the genuine one that rolled so easily, the laugh that was infectious to everyone around her—could be heard clearly throughout the room. When heads turned, she became embarrassed, her cheeks tinged with pink, and her eyes lowered, but she was still laughing inside.

She stole another glance at him, but he was shuffling cards, looking bored and even a bit melancholy. Something about him reminded Becky of a scarecrow, those homemade men with straw sticking out from under discarded hats, arms and legs made of slats.

They played a lively game of Rook, with hardly a word from Daniel. He simply laid his cards, with an occasional smile, but the expression of relaxed boredom stayed. Elam, however, proved to be a good player—smart, witty, and quick to speak his mind—and Becky became increasingly intrigued by this nice-looking, well-spoken young man.

Her birthday party, however, taught her a lesson about the group of youth in her Wisconsin community. She had found someone attractive, but this young man was not attracted to her, but to the willowy Lydia. The attention paid to her cousin seemed constant; she was endlessly being noticed, while Becky remained consistently in the background.

Oh, everyone was friendly and nice. Not once did anyone speak rudely or in a way that made her feel self-conscious. She just wasn't there, if you observed many of the boys.

Becky got it. She was not slow to learn, but quick-witted, aware of the attitudes of others, and a good

judge of character. And too overweight to be completely attractive. She was coming to accept this.

Her friends were numerous. She genuinely enjoyed her weekends and learned not to expect much
from anyone. So she got along well.

When winter rode in on a steady wind, bringing intense cold, farm life slowed down to the point that
Becky learned to sew. She made a blue cotton dress
out of an old piece of fabric which Mam allowed her
to cut and sew, for practice. She proved to be quite
a seamstress, bent over the Bernina sewing machine,
working the treadle with her strong legs, producing
a wearable dress in a few hours with only a few questions for Mam.

She learned to bake and decorate birthday cakes
from a book of ideas she found at the local library.
She produced moist chocolate cakes and iced them
to perfection with her own recipe of buttercream
frosting, then dotted the tops and sides with carefully sculpted roses, leaves, scallops, or daisies, all of
which she made.

Word got around, the way these things do, and before long she had an order almost every week. Her cakes were creations of beauty and great flavor.

Mam was rife with praise. Becky's eyes sparkled with gratitude, loving her mother for every generous word, and gladly accepting kind words from Nancy as well.

Her life was good; she was blessed beyond what she deserved. She filled her journal with words of thanksgiving and gratefulness to God. She had become a good hired hand, seamstress, and baker. And she could sing.

When Becky sang, her voice came from deep in her throat, rich, full, and vibrant, sending chills down her listeners' spines. She loved to sing. She could remember every hymn from school and only had to listen to a song once or twice before she could sing it perfectly, imitating any song from the radio or wherever she happened to hear it.

She started many songs at the youth's hymn-singings, unaware of the impact her own beautiful voice had on many of the parents who sat in the room with the young people. "Oh, *selly Becky kann singa,*" they said, shaking their heads. Too bad she didn't try and lose some of that weight, they said. She could have anyone she wanted.

That winter when she turned sixteen, Becky was happy and truly content, until—in quite a short amount of time—she wasn't. The barn chores were cold and dirty, the ice packed around the doors a nuisance. Dat worked on her nerves with his endless, low whistling. She didn't want to sew or bake cakes. Even her weekends were cold and filled with endless snow, with nothing to do but play Rook or ping-pong or sit at the long table and sing on Sunday evenings.

Lydia was asked out on a Sunday evening by Elam Fisher, the charming, brown-haired boy with freckles scattered over his tanned skin. He asked her for a real date, so of course that left Becky alone, without being able to lean on her best friend and favorite cousin.

Becky shrugged her shoulders inwardly, warding off the ghost of despondency by not caring, the answer for all of life's ills. Outwardly, she gave all the expected congratulations, squealing, hugging Lydia, the forced gladness in her eyes disguised as real joy.

Even Mam and Nancy thought Becky was admirable, the way she was genuinely happy for her cousin. What they didn't know was that Becky was lying in her room, a Kleenex stuffed to her nose, her eyelids trembling with tears, as she wrestled with the disappointment of having her friend join the daters.

Now what? She'd have to be with Rachel and Linda, those other sixteen-year-olds who would accept her only because they had no other choice.

Suddenly, the world seemed big and scary as she floundered in the choppy waters of her own making. No one would ask her to be his girlfriend. She was too young. And large. No one would want her; no one would care if Lydia dated without her.

She sat up suddenly, wiped her eyes, and told herself that this was enough of this stuff right now. Wallowing in her misery like a pig in its slop would not get her anywhere. (She cringed at the likeness.)

She would go out and get a job. She wanted to work in the kitchen of a restaurant. She would learn to cook. Every day she would wear a white bib apron—so English, she thought—and she would be a cook in a big, clean kitchen at a restaurant. Some Amish girls did.

So she asked her parents, meeting the disappointment in Dat's eyes, the fear and mistrust in Mam's, her brothers' surprise, and Nancy's indifference. She let it all roll off her back like water on a duck and pressed on, saying she needed a challenge.

Dat said the challenge she needed was spring arriving with all the fieldwork. Mam said a restaurant kitchen was no place for an Amish girl. Her brothers came right out and said she didn't realize how hard it would be cooking in a restaurant, getting all those scribbled orders at one time. Nancy said she didn't know the first thing about cooking anywhere but in a home, and what was wrong with staying right here on the farm helping Dat?

Becky felt irritation rise in her throat like acid, and she chose not to suppress it. She told her family it simply wasn't right if she wasn't permitted to try, since everyone else was allowed to experiment with new things, to go out and see what they could find, to get off the farm and get a job.

In the end, they said okay. Becky got her wish—employment at a local eatery, a restaurant known for its home-style cooking, called simply "Fred's Diner."

By the time the biggest snowfall of the year arrived, Becky was lifting oblong baskets of French fries from the hot oil, flipping burgers, and learning the art of getting along with her coworkers. They were all English, diligent, and not too crazy about having to work with this inexperienced young Amish girl.

Fred was hard to work for, they said. Keep your head down and your opinions to yourself. He always knows more than you do. So Becky did what they told her.

CHAPTER 3

SHE WAS OBEDIENT, TRUE TO THE TEACHING SHE learned at home. In spite of complicated orders that were scrawled haphazardly on too small pages of the waitress order book, Becky not only survived, she flourished.

She was extremely fast with her hands. Multitasking came naturally for her. She flipped burgers as if she had been doing it all her life, kicked refrigerator doors closed with one foot when her hands were full of ingredients. She whirled and twirled about the greasy kitchen behind the swinging doors, stained along the edges by years of hands and trays bumping them open.

At first Fred had been a lot more disagreeable than he was now. He was small and swarthy, his skin pocked with old acne scars, his dark hair combed in perfect ridges across his head. Dark sideburns grew low on his face; his small black eyes darted busily, missing nothing. He ran a tight ship, the waitresses warned, but to Becky, it was no different than hard work on the farm, especially on sweltering days when Dat's temper ran short.

Becky worked on the grill, that smooth, hot piece of tempered steel that had been greased so often it resembled black ice. She learned fast, knowing which section was for things done in a hot pan, and which foods were done over low heat. She handled the fryer, chopped food, and prepared meat, until one day Fred actually paid her a compliment, saying she was doing a great job. Then he frowned immediately and told her to wipe the counters down with Clorox.

There was one waitress, however, who made her job as miserable as she could. Her name was Kit, short for Katrina. With short, spiked, black hair, a complexion as dented as a walnut shell, numerous tattoos, and an attitude like frozen meat, she evaluated Becky on her first day with a long, frank stare from beneath half-closed lids and sneered, "Whatever."

Kit never fazed Becky. She decided she was the most worldly person she had ever encountered, so she'd leave her alone, the way you respected a porcupine and its quills. As long as Becky stayed in the kitchen and Kit waited on tables, she could overlook her snide remarks about her clothes, her weight, and her Amish practices.

But then, the small blue slips that hung above the grill, with the orders scrawled across them in barely legible handwriting, became completely undecipherable. Turkey tracks would have been as informative.

As the orders piled up, Becky became completely bewildered. She caught Fred's attention and voiced her complaint.

In disbelief, she soaked up the scathing words of her employer, who told her that was the trouble with the Amish—they never went to high school—so figure it out.

She couldn't. She had no idea what those scrawls meant, so how was she supposed to cook? Unbidden, her lower lip trembled, and she swallowed back a lump of defeat.

Just as unexpectedly, a quick flush of anger suffused her face. This was unfair. It wasn't right. Fred was not going to do this to her, making her feel like she was a nobody, a dumb, uneducated Amish girl. She had rights, same as everyone else, and he was not getting away with this.

She walked after him, calling his name in a loud, firm voice. He turned, his eyes half-closed with displeasure. Becky thrust the orders at him, a handful of small blue papers covered with chicken scratches.

"Here, you can cook. I quit. This is no way to treat anyone, Amish, English, anyone."

With that, she grabbed her purse from the hook, and without looking back, marched solidly through the back door, past the greasy, stinking Dumpsters, between Fred's flashy truck and Kit's scroungy-looking Honda with the bumper off on one side. She turned right and walked the entire four miles home without a trace of guilt. Her coat kept her warm, and the air was crisp and invigorating. She wore good shoes, so her walk was actually a pleasure.

What had she been thinking?

The diner was no place for her. The stale air, the poorly lit kitchen, the endless sizzling of grease; she was glad to be out of the place.

She laughed aloud, thinking of Fred's bulging eyes and the disbelief on Kit's face as she pushed past her. Nope. Not a place for her.

As she walked in the driveway, the farm looked solid, plain, even a bit stark with the maples stripped of their leaves. But it was okay. It was home, a place where people were kind. Even Nancy would have helped her decipher those words. Anyone would have. She hoped Fred had a hard time finding a cook to replace her.

So here she was. Best friend dating and no job. With a nice crop of acne on her face because of the unhealthy food. And no prospects of another job. Well, she'd take a day at a time and see what occurred.

What did occur in the following weeks was nothing. Nothing at all. With winter coming on, the farm work slowed to a crawl. Dat attended horse sales and cow auctions. The house contained no oxygen for Becky, or so it seemed. The four walls surrounding her stifled her breathing, as if they meant to collapse at any minute.

Nancy irritated her, the boys ignored her, and Mam was prickly that Christmas was coming so fast and she was barely finished housecleaning. Becky's "Now ain't that somepin'" was on the tip of her tongue, but she was wiser than her years and knew better than to say that when Mam was in a dither.

She milked cows twice a day with Dat, the only time she felt any sense of fulfillment. She loved the cows. One elbow propped on a cow's back, she stood and watched the way their long, coarse tongues gathered up the vinegary silage, their heads moving efficiently as the milkers chugged beneath them, extracting the warm, frothy milk into the shining, stainless steel bucket.

Dat whistled low under his breath or hummed nameless tunes that surrounded Becky with security. Dat was content in the cow stable, and easy. He required nothing of Becky except her companionship. If no one spoke, that was fine with him, and if Becky did start a conversation, that was fine with him as well. He'd bend his head slightly and shift the long piece of hay in his mouth. Fine lines would appear at the side of his eyes as his face smiled only a bit. He'd nod, the lines would deepen, then he'd laugh outright or shake his head, depending on the nature of her words.

He knew his Becky was different. She was not like the boys or Nancy. She viewed the world with the brilliant light of her own humor and sharp wit. She was no dummy, his Becky. He'd watch her short, solid form wash the milkers with intense concentration, water and soap up to her elbows, the low whine of the cooling unit on the bulk tank accompanying her as she burst into song.

He would stop and hold as still as a hawk waiting to dive for a fish, his ears taking in the unbelievable sound of his daughter's voice. Tears always rushed to his eyes as chills suffused his body. No matter what she sang—hymns, school songs, or a modern song she heard on the radio—her voice carried a tremor, a full-throated, wondrous gift that God bestowed on only a few.

Becky sang lustily at her job washing milkers. She pretended she was onstage and let her voice soar with her mind. When she lifted the heavy buckets from the rinse water, she threw back her head and let her voice rise, unaware of the fact that she brought her father to tears.

She would never be onstage. She would never be allowed. She was an Amish girl, and performing was severely frowned upon. But no one could stop her in the milk house. Here she was in her own domain. If one of her brothers opened a door and came in, it was like punching the power button on an electronic device. Off immediately.

She finished cleaning the milk house floor, hung the broom on the peg by its rawhide loop, and tip-toed across the wet floor, back into the cow stable to see if Dat had finished.

Catching sight of him, she yelled, "You done?"

"You mind sweeping the troughs?" he yelled back.

"No."

Becky grabbed the stiff-bristled push broom, sweeping the silage tidily within reach of the cows' eager snuffling. She swallowed, hungry now, antici-pating her own breakfast. She hoped Mam would fry scrapple. It was so good with stewed crackers and homemade ketchup.

When she stepped outside, she was surprised to see low scudding clouds hiding the sun. Or most of it. Oops. Snow, Becky thought.

When gray clouds gave the sun the appearance of a distant flashlight, and a circle of color slightly brighter than the gray surrounded it, snow or rain was coming, depending on the season. Well, that was good. Christmas wasn't far away, so she hoped there'd be snow. Perhaps it would stay cold, and they'd have a white Christmas this year.

The kitchen smelled wonderful. Becky swallowed as she washed her hands and peered into the oval mirror above the small sink in the *Kesslehaus*. Turning her face this way and that, she scrutinized the angry red pustules marching along her jawline. Instantly, her hand went up and her fingertips traced the raised bumps on her jaw. Leaning forward, she turned her head to find the offending yellowish tip of a pimple, squeezed as hard as she could, then drew in a sharp breath with the intensity of the pain as tears sprang to her eyes.

Ouchie, ouchie, she thought. It was all that grease in the kitchen at Fred's. But why now?

Mam eyed her closely as she entered the kitchen. "Becky, have you been picking at your pimples again? How often do I have to tell you you're only making the situation worse?"

In her frustration, Mam slopped a yellow puddle of orange juice on the white tablecloth. "Get a towel."

Becky reached for a paper towel, handed it to her mother, and went to put slices of bread in the broiler pan without being told. There was always that, her sense of foresight, her ability to manage jobs in the kitchen, that pleased her mother.

As she turned to heat the coffee, she rubbed her fingertips along the side of her face, as if to obliterate the offending bumps from Mam's eyesight.

She ate methodically, bending her head over her plate as she shoveled large portions of the delicious fried eggs, scrapple, and stewed crackers into her mouth. Bites of toast spread with butter and strawberry jam were pure ambrosia.

"No pancakes?"

Mam shook her head. "Shoofly."

Dat said there was nothing better than fresh shoofly pie with his morning coffee. Nancy sniffed and went to the refrigerator for her container of Chobani vanilla yogurt, mixed with birdseed, as Becky called her minimal amount of Kashi granola. She had eaten one egg and one piece of dry toast before she tackled the unappetizing mix she daintily nibbled on now.

What a letdown it would be to eat like Nancy. Greek yogurt was disgusting. It tasted the way the used milk filters smelled, as they stuck to the side of the green garbage bag in the trash can placed beside the sink in the milk house.

She eyed the shoofly pie, then cut herself a sizable wedge, placing it carefully in a cereal bowl.

"Milk," she said.

Mam handed her the small ceramic pitcher of milk, and she poured a steady stream over the pie until it was almost covered. Holding her spoon vertically, she cut off the tip of the wedge, turned it so that the milk would soak into the cakey part, then took a large bite with satisfaction. Not quite as good as pancakes soaked with butter and syrup, but far better than yogurt and granola.

"So, Becky, what are your plans for today?" Dat asked.

Becky's hand went to the angry red pustules on her face, as if anyone addressing her would be talking to them. "I don't know."

"Nancy and I are going shopping in Concord. Would you want to go, too?" Mam asked, leaning back in her chair.

Becky's hand stayed on her jawline. "I'd have to get money from my savings."

"Did you spend everything you made at the diner?"

Becky nodded.

"On what? My word."

"Books."

"What kind of books?"

"Books I like."

"Well, what kind, I meant. Christian stories? Books that build character? Or just trashy romance novels without morals that are not good for your soul?" Mam sipped her coffee, her eyes narrowed as she searched her daughter's face.

"Interesting books. Stories that hold my attention. Real life. Worthwhile stories."

Becky breathed again when Mam let it go.

The truth was, Becky had discovered a whole new, colorful world when she began reading books that captivated her attention. History, classics written in the twenties and thirties by authors who were long gone but used words and sentence structures in an entirely new way. Nancy glanced at her sharply, scraped out the last of her yogurt, and said, "You need to do something worthwhile during the day."

"You need another job," Mam chimed in.

"Find me one."

Dat cleared his throat. "Why does she need one if she helps milk, feed calves, and does other chores? She's so good in the barn, I don't know why she needs to be pressured to find a job."

Mam nodded, smiling. "I know what you're saying, Enos. But you heard her. She spent her money. Now she has to get into her savings account to go shopping for Christmas. If she had a job, that would not be necessary."

"I'll provide money for her to go shopping."

Becky picked at her chin, her eyes going from her father's face to her mother's.

"She's worth more to me than all the boys, who go out and get a job after they turn sixteen. Nothing wrong with that either—they need to experience the world—but I'm just saying, if Becky wants to help around the farm, she can."

"But in winter?" Mam protested.

"She works two hours every morning and evening. That's four hours. That is a job."

So Becky cashed a two-hundred-dollar check at the bank in Concord and went shopping with Mam and Nancy. The stores were festive with holiday finery and alive with Christmas music, piped in through speakers somewhere on the wall.

They went to Target, to Walmart, and Tractor Supply. They bought gifts for their grandparents, each other, the boys, the boss at market. They shopped for necessities as well. Thick stockings, wool socks, and underwear for the boys; Muck Boots for Dat, along with heavy shirts and long thermal underwear.

Becky was hungry to the point of collapse till Mam finally asked the surly, overweight driver to stop at McDonald's, which instantly elevated his disposition to the point of being quite talkative.

Going to McDonald's was a rare treat for Becky, as going out to eat was deemed simply unnecessary, *unedich gelt chpent*. Thrift was a virtue, and Amish people should eat at home, Mam fully believed. But at Christmas, they would indulge in the pleasure of a Big Mac or a chicken sandwich accompanied by a large cardboard container of the best fries on Earth.

Becky's goodwill escalated right along with the driver's. She praised Nancy's choice of a black sweater she purchased at Target and became quite affable with Mam, who returned her smile with one of her own.

However, the TV mounted in the corner of the restaurant distracted Becky to such a degree that she forgot where she was for a short time. When an ad came on showing the disfigured face of a young teenaged girl, followed by the same girl with a creamy, smooth complexion after using a product called "Proactive," Becky's mind went on high alert, memorizing the number to call immediately. She rummaged in her purse, came up with a small notepad and ballpoint pen, and scribbled the number as fast as she could.

Mam raised her eyebrows. Nancy asked outright.

Becky pointed to the TV. "Something for my face." She added, "Wish Amish people had TVs."

That stirred up the soup in a satisfactory way. Mam's eyebrows came down, followed by a snort of disapproval and a firm, "Becky!" while Nancy's eyelids were lowered to half-mast, with a pitying, charitable version of patience written all over her face.

"Really, how childish."

"It's not childish. Some shows are informative."

"How would you know?"

"The diner."

"Oh."

"I could always get a cell phone, I guess."

That was like rocking the whole soup bowl until it sloshed over the sides and ran onto the floor, where it dripped like scalding coffee on Mam's shoes.

"You're not serious!" Nancy sputtered.

Mam looked as if she was trying to swallow a balloon, so Becky hastily assured her she was only kidding. You'd think she had asked to be flown to the moon.

Becky ate three fries in one bite, wiped the ketch-up off her fingers, and reached for more. She pulled deeply on the plastic straw stuck into her large choco-late milkshake, marveling at the wondrous concoc-tion made with milk and ice cream. She shoved a large portion of her burger into her mouth and chewed, returning Mam's level gaze with one of her own. She watched Nancy squeeze some of the gluey purple dressing onto her Asian salad, pick up her fork, and convey a small amount to her mouth deli-cately, holding her fork with finesse. Whatever that meant. It was a word she had read somewhere, mean-ing something like expertly fancy. That's what Nancy was, all right—classy.

Mam was in between. Not classy, really. Just ordi-nary. Eating a fish sandwich with coffee and cream. Perhaps she'd go back and order a small hot fudge sundae if the line wasn't too long.

Becky's spirits rose with the level of her blood sugar, the milkshake giving her a real high. Gather-ing the handles of her large black purse, she trilled, "Well, I'm off to the cell phone place!" Then she laughed aloud, chuckling to herself the whole way to the van, which was bulging with bags and boxes of Christmas items.

On the backseat on the way home, Becky began to regret her behavior at McDonald's, questioning her own motives. Why was it so tempting to horrify Mam and Nancy?

She felt ashamed of herself and made plans to read her Bible that evening, then ask God to forgive her rebelliousness. Mam and Nancy were so perfect, that was the thing. So admiring of one another. They oohed and aahed about the same item—some candle or bedspread or rug or set of dishes—never asking what she thought.

It was as if she really wasn't there. She didn't rate very high on the scale of mattering. In plain words, she, or her opinion, *didn't* matter. Who cared what she thought? And if she did voice an opinion, it was the wrong one, so she kept quiet, or like at McDonald's, said rude and ignorant things and ate all the wrong food.

Again, Becky had to tap into her reserve of self-acceptance. She didn't really care what they thought either. This thing could work both ways.

Then, since it was Christmas, and because that milkshake still served the purpose of keeping her spirits high, Becky smiled and noticed the Christmas trees and tinsel, the snowmen on porches, Santa Claus and his reindeer in the yards.

She was filled with happiness when the first few snowflakes hit the windshield. Her Christmas spirit widened as the driver flicked the knob to begin the windshield wipers, and the surrounding countryside looked as if someone had powdered it lightly with 10X sugar, like covered filled doughnuts. The atmosphere was gray and so heavy with snow that it turned blue-white, bits of snow zapping the windshield like millions of dust particles.

The driver gripped the steering wheel, grumbling to himself. Mam glanced over but said nothing. Nancy turned her head to the right, nervously chewing her lip. Becky remembered the Almond Joy candy bar in her purse. Better leave it.

She had just turned back to the window when she felt the van shudder, as if it had run over a giant comb. The driver shouted and hit the brakes. For one moment time stood still as Becky realized he had lost control of the vehicle. There was a hard jolt, a few bumps, and the van came to rest at an angle, halfway into a shallow ditch, with the snow coming down as steadily as before.

"Slippy. Road's slippy," was all the driver said. He climbed out, took stock of his situation, and scratched his balding head before opening the door and asking if they would mind giving him a bit of a shove.

Mam immediately said they'd be glad to help. Nancy sniffed and rolled her eyes at the driver's incompetence, but she said nothing. Becky got out and leaned her strength against the hood of the van as the driver put it in reverse. A few good spins of the tires, and they got nowhere.

The driver called, "Don't exert yourselves. I'll call AAA."

Becky waved him away. "We'll get it out. Keep trying. Nancy, you help Mam on this corner, and I'll push against the opposite side. One, two, three. PUSH!"

Becky's face turned red with her mighty effort. The driver spun the wheels as the engine screamed over and over. Then there was a lurch, the crunch of gravel, and the solid thump of the back wheels hitting macadam. A car stopped, its four-ways blinking like cat eyes through the snow. A portly gentleman clad in a brilliant blue coat asked if they needed help.

"Nope. We're out," the driver said proudly for having taken care of the situation without outside help.

They crept home slowly after that, with Mam clutching the arm of the seat, her eyes never leaving the windshield, the oncoming traffic appearing like ghostly machines of death to her.

Nancy leaned over to fix her hair and covering in the rearview mirror.

Becky reached into her purse, unwrapped the Almond Joy, and ate both succulent pieces in two bites. Good thing she had weight and strength when something like this came along. She felt very pleased as she crumpled the wrapper.

CHAPTER 4

AND SO THE CHRISTMAS SEASON BEGAN IN EAR-nest. Mam and the girls opened long cardboard rolls of brightly colored Christmas wrap and showed each other the gifts they had bought, fussing over them one by one. Then they stuck them back in their boxes and covered them in red wrapping paper, or blue, with snowmen, greens, or candy canes, but never with images of Santa Claus. That was just not something the Amish believed in, same as Halloween and all its imaginary witches and ghosts and goblins. If a Christmas wrap was adorned with the jolly face of Santa, it was put back, and a poinsettia motif might be chosen instead.

The women started their candy production. Mam cooked fudge and made Rice Krispies Treats. They made all the candy during the day when the four boys were at work, or else, Mam said, the confections would be eaten as fast as they finished them.

Becky sat on a kitchen chair with boxes of Ritz Crackers and a six-pound container of Jif peanut butter, working her way down the tubes of crackers. She spread a glob of peanut butter between two crackers, then placed each sandwich on a tray, ready for Nancy to dunk them into the bowl of melted chocolate. Nancy dipped each one, turned it with a fork, then fished it out, shaking off the excess chocolate with a few firm taps of the fork handle on the side of the bowl.

Tap, tap, tap. Nancy kept coating the crackers, her eyes heavy from lack of sleep. It was Monday. The hymn-singing on Sunday night had run on endlessly, and she still had not been asked out on a real date by the highly esteemed but slippery Allen Kauffman.

Nancy's mood meter was controlled completely by the amount of time she spent with him, the sentences they spoke, the looks they exchanged, and whether she had ridden with him in his new buggy. His carriage was upholstered in gray and silver paisley and had a cherry-colored glove compartment with more gadgets and doodads then any buggy Nancy had ever known.

A long ride in that buggy equaled a smiling Nancy on Monday morning. All her conversation threatened to sink into giddiness, and she was willing to help with even the meanest chores. But if she and Allen had barely talked and she had had no buggy ride, Monday morning meant sleepiness, yawning, and a general lack of enthusiasm.

When Allen Kauffman hadn't been around at all, Nancy had long and serious conversations in the kitchen with Mam, after which her eyebrows would be raised, the anxiety in her voice pushing them to their limits. On those days, Becky rated about as high as a spider on the ceiling.

Today, as far as Becky could tell, the mood meter indicated that Allen had offered a greeting, maybe a sentence or two, but no conversation and, most assuredly, no buggy ride. Becky slapped peanut butter on two Ritz Crackers and squeezed them together, resisting the urge to lick the excess and return the crackers to the tray without telling anyone.

Mam was stirring a pot on the stove, her movements jerky, her eyebrows about three-fourths of the way to a nervous breakdown. Boredom needed to be dispelled, Becky decided.

Launching the million-dollar question, she asked Nancy if she knew Allen had taken Rachel Ann to the singing.

Nancy's head swiveled like a whip. "Who?"

"Rachel Ann."

"You mean, he *asked* her? And just the two of them went together?"

"Oh no, Jesse and David and Sarah Mae went, too."

"Well, say what you mean, Becky. I thought you meant he took her alone."

"What would you do if he did?"

Nancy arranged her face into a caricature of unconcern, expertly gathering her pride and hiding it behind her eyes, the way she always did.

"I guess then it would be God's will, Becky. You know, choosing a boyfriend is a spiritual matter. We have to let God rule our lives in matters of the heart, same as everything else. You'll learn that yet as you grow older."

Becky caught Mam's look of pure adoration, admiring her oldest daughter to the point of worship. "That's so true, Nancy. You can't go wrong, placing your trust in God the way you do."

A slow burn began somewhere in a region of Becky's mind, which turned into a light that flamed in her eyes. She actually did try to keep quiet for about five seconds, but in the end she said evenly, "Yes, it is always good to have that kind of faith, Nancy," knowing it was the only thing that would be acceptable in that anxious kitchen.

So Nancy had a strong faith and no will. That was always good, now, wasn't it? Well, she hoped things would turn out well for Mam and Nancy and that Allen would come around and ask her, but it wouldn't surprise her if it didn't happen.

What did Nancy know about giving up? She lived in the realm of Mam's approval, with adoring brothers, a boy's admiration, and a good job. She had no clue what it meant to give up before you even started.

Becky couldn't put it into words. She just knew what it meant to accept the fact that she was still on the bottom rung of the ladder of popularity, and that she'd likely never climb to even the second or third rungs. Recognizing that took giving up. But here was the thing. If she suggested as much to Mam and Nancy, they'd hoot her right out of the kitchen.

So she kept her peace like a round little owl, watching and blinking and thinking her thoughts.

The two oldest boys, Aaron and Abner, worked for North Wisconsin Roofing. With the recent snowfall, they shoveled snow off flat roofs, finishing just before noon. So they ate their lunches and came home.

Mam met them at the laundry room door and asked them to please hang their wet things in the basement by the woodstove. Obediently, they clumped down the stairs.

Quickly, Mam hid some of the fudge and hurriedly whipped the Rice Krispies Treats behind the pantry door. But there was nothing to be done about the chocolate-coated crackers.

The boys fell on them with glee, scooping up five or six each, then sprawling on kitchen chairs and teasing Nancy unmercifully, which produced only a regal bearing and a mask of pride from her.

"How come you weren't in Allen's load, good sister? You must have gotten lost somewhere. Did you know he's going to Tioga next weekend?"

Becky winced. Ouch.

All of Nancy's resolve fell away, melting off her like candle wax. Up shot her eyebrows as her face lost color, fading like evening light. "What does he want there? Did he say?"

The boy's faces were alive with interest, driving Nancy straight into an unabashed dither.

"He didn't say, I don't believe. As far as *wanting* something, I couldn't say. He didn't mention names at all."

Quickly, Nancy gathered herself, turned her back, and busied herself at the counter.

Aaron and Abner raised their eyebrows and laughed aloud, clearly enjoying Nancy's discomfort.

Becky kept on spreading peanut butter, observing all of this without comment. She felt a sort of displaced sympathy, weak and filmy, but she did care, nevertheless. It must be awfully hard work, keeping up that queenly image, she mused. The princess of pride. Well, what goes up must come down, she reasoned, and so it would probably be.

Today she found herself hoping Allen would ask her sister. Her own *rumschpringa* was a source of amusement, actually. Now at Christmastime, especially. There were endless rounds of places to go and things to do, so naturally she had come to know the youth better than ever.

Tonight a group of the young people were going caroling at Round Oaks Elder Care, a small, local facility for the aging and infirm, elderly people who needed special care. Some were bedridden or not capable of speaking or walking, often crippled with rheumatoid arthritis or worse.

Becky had never been there, but Nancy had told her about it, saying it was hard to visit, but how much it meant to these elderly folks when you spoke a few words to them and wished them well.

Becky put on her red Christmas dress, fresh off the sewing machine, which she had hemmed and pressed all by herself. She was proud of that dress, especially the sleeves, which she had made so neatly

with a plain cuff, then pressed with a wet handkerchief and a sad iron, which the Amish used as a kind
of steam iron. It worked like a charm.

She felt good about her hair as she sprayed it lib-
erally with her Fructis hairspray. I may be large, she
thought, but I can comb my hair along with the best.
Her covering was white and crisp, her face glowing
with excitement.

She sighed, feeling her jawline for the dreaded
bumps. Turning her head, she viewed them in the
glaring light of the battery lamp. Horrible. Just awful. Like a dinosaur's skin.

She groaned. No one would want to stand beside her, and certainly not touch her, not even brush
against her sleeve. Everyone would ask what was
wrong with her face. Poison ivy? Not in winter. Mea-
sles? Nope.

She clenched her fists and opened her mouth,
letting loose a wail of despair that brought Nancy
pounding down the hall.

"Whatever, Becky?"

"My face!"

"I noticed."

"What can I do? It's so disgusting. No one will want to stand beside me to sing. It's like I have rabies or mange. Like a coon or a possum Dat and the boys would shoot."

Becky was surprised to hear her sister laugh whole-heartedly.

"No one's going to shoot you."

"Well."

"Let me get you my medicated covering lotion. And powder."

Becky went straight to the mirror to examine the horrible red pimples, almost in tears when Nancy returned.

"Hold still." She held Becky's face, swabbed the offending marks with a cool cloth, then applied a cream with her fingers, lightly patting the affected area.

"Don't tell Mam I have face powder, okay?" Nancy said. "She hates this stuff. Thinks it's makeup, which it isn't, really. It just covers things when there's an emergency, like now."

She giggled, turned Becky's face, and said, "Now look."

Becky's eyes opened wide and a broad smile creased her face, revealing the two dimples in her round cheeks. "Nancy, I can't believe it!"

"Only for emergencies, Becky. Promise?"

"I promise."

Nancy stayed, watching Becky adjust her covering. Becky glanced at her in the mirror. "Oh, I forgot. Thank you."

Nancy waved her away. "I just wanted you to know that you look very pretty in your Christmas dress. I guess I feel clumsy giving you a compliment. I don't believe I ever have."

Her face took on a tenderness, a softening. "You really are the cutest, roundest little thing."

Becky turned and, without thinking, threw her arms around her sister, giving her such a hefty squeeze that she heard Nancy's breath leaving in an astounded whoosh.

Stepping back, Becky's eyes were wet with tears, and her mouth wobbled only a bit. "Ain't that somepin', Nancy! You mean it, don't you?"

Nancy nodded, whereupon Becky flung her arms around her sister a second time, with the same muscular clamp that surprised Nancy again.

"Thank you, thank you. That's what sisters are for. And, Becky, I'm sorry for the times I insulted you. I have to realize God made us very different, and I need to accept you just the way you are. And I do."

Round Oaks Elder Care was only about six miles from the Enos Esh farm, but Nancy and Becky bounced around back roads picking up lots of the youth until the fifteen-passenger van was filled to capacity. Close to an hour later, they turned off Route 433, the main road into the town of Waverley, and followed a wide, winding driveway up to a long, low, brick building. It had a wide porch along the front, with white pillars wrapped in festive lights and a lengthy row of windows decorated with evergreen wreaths.

The combination of the snow on the roof and the Christmas tree with colorful lights delighted Becky. She thought this would surely be one of the nicest places on Earth to spend your final days. Curious and eager, she piled out of the van with the six girls and eight boys. She noticed Allen Kauffman's absence and felt genuinely sorry for Nancy now.

They were greeted by the other youth group who had arrived with their driver. They immediately distributed songbooks and made their way to the front door. A smiling English woman wearing a brilliant red dress and black high heels ushered them inside.

"Welcome to Round Oaks. We're happy to have you. Come this way, please."

The room they entered was pleasant and well lit with high ceilings, low comfortable chairs and couches, thick rugs, and cozy lamps. The Christmas tree gave off a warm holiday glow. The scent of spiced pinecones hung in the air. What a lovely place, Becky thought again.

As the woman marched them into a narrow hallway, the scent of pinecones evaporated, replaced by a nose-burning, indistinguishable odor that left Becky bewildered. What was that smell? Doors to her left were flung open, showing another welcoming, well lit room, filled with Christmas cheer, another tree, and warm shaded lamps casting a cozy yellow glow on the carpeting, and again, the invigorating scent of pinecones.

Becky blinked, then blinked again, adjusting her eyes to the various forms seated on chairs and a few on wheelchairs. All their heads were bowed, all with white hair, some sparse and balding, with age spots like flecks of dirt or sand. A few of the men lifted their heads, their eyes alert and knowing, as they studied these Amish youth who had come to sing.

The tall woman in red clapped her hands, asked for attention and duly received it, as all heads lifted obediently like well behaved classmates in a schoolroom.

Becky was unprepared for the quick rush of pity she felt, her sudden wish to hold these people's hands and beg to hear their stories. Why were they here? Did they want to be here? Were they happy? Did they have a spouse? Children? Were they allowed pets?

Oh, she wanted to know. She wanted to find out about their lives, listen to their stories, wipe their tears, bring them a Kleenex or a cold drink of water. Or perhaps they preferred juice.

Once when Mam was in the hospital to have a hernia repaired, the nurse brought her a snack in the evening. Graham crackers with peanut butter and cold apple juice. The snack tasted so good, it made Becky feel snug and warm. Mam had let her eat most of it, and she kept eating the very same thing at home for weeks afterward.

Tonight her mind was not on the Christmas songs as she observed the elderly with a keen gaze. She noticed the emotion on one woman's face, the look of enjoyment on another, the tapping of gnarly old fingers keeping time on the arm of a wheelchair upholstered in blue leather. She wondered if they had children, family who came to visit. Were they allowed to leave, to go home for Christmas dinner? Did they still have another home?

She watched the attendants. One rotund woman was dressed in the same clothes as the dentist's hygienist, wearing a loose wrap around top and pressed polyester pants, just like a nurse. Her hair was dyed an unnatural shade of jet black; her face was puffy and pale, without expression. She reached down to adjust a lap robe and to place a helpless foot on a footrest, patting a shoulder and smiling as she did so. She was definitely not unkind—just detached, yet good at her job.

How many caregivers were here? How many residents? Or did you call them patients, like in a hospital?

The singing stopped. Becky felt an elbow in her side and jumped. She looked up to find Daniel looking down at her.

"Your turn."

"What?"

"Your turn."

Confused, Becky looked up to find Daniel's eyes almost closed by his full grin.

"You were so busy checking out these old folks, you were barely singing."

That irked Becky. What she was doing was none of his business. Why was he worried about what she was looking at? Duh.

She told him so in a fierce whisper. She was glad to see him wince and turn his head. She hated for him to see her observing these aging people. He had probably even noticed the tears she tried so hard to keep from forming. The pity she felt was hers alone and not his concern. He could act so superior. But she had put him in his place, now hadn't she?

They sang on. Becky led "What Child Is This?" aware of Daniel's deep alto voice above hers. Now that she knew he was standing so close, she kept her eyes on the words of the song and tried to put the elderly residents from her mind.

They were served red punch in tiny, thin glasses. A tray of crackers and cheese was passed around, with small red napkins featuring a picture of Santa Claus printed in white.

"Miss."

Becky turned.

"Miss?" An elderly gentleman crooked a forefinger in her direction, beckoning her.

Quickly Becky went over to him and sat down on a folding chair at his side. He reached for her hand and shook it, his hand cold and dry and papery, but with a grasp that was soft. He continued holding her hand, which Becky allowed, hoping Daniel was occupied elsewhere.

The old man's mouth shook visibly as he strained to control his voice. "Your voice, Miss, is like a bell. You sound like, well, you wouldn't know her, but you bring to mind the quality of Aretha Franklin's voice."

Becky smiled, shaking her head. "I don't know her."

The old man smiled. "No, you wouldn't."

Releasing her hand, he patted her arm, telling her she had a gift, the gift of song.

"Thank you."

That was the proper thing, wasn't it? To say thank you when an English person paid you a compliment. She had earlier told Nancy thank you, too. She took this very seriously, receiving two compliments in the course of one evening.

The old man was so thin his shirt hung loose on his wide shoulders that spoke of strength in the past. His hair was sparse, white with an underlying tone of gray. His eyes were blue, almost hidden in folds of skin that had surrounded those eyes for many decades. His face had felt the sun and the wind and the rain during a time when the world had been simpler and calmer, the air not as polluted, the ozone layer still healthy, the atmosphere crisp and pure. There had been little technology, probably TV only in black and white. There was segregation in the South and only a handful of Amish communities compared to what there was now.

The deep wrinkles that lined his cheeks spoke of his old age, the trembling mouth of his receding strength. Becky's eyes took in the creases and folds of his face, the large old hands with knobs of arthritis disfiguring his long fingers. His wrists were so thin and bony that the blue cuffs of his shirt appeared oversized.

When he spoke, Becky did not know what to say.

"Your voice touched me deeply. I hope you will come back to visit us soon. My name is Harold Epstein. My wife passed away in 2006, so I've been here for four years."

He paused, his hand trembling on Becky's sleeve. "I have two daughters, Joanne and Julie, but they both live abroad, one in Rome, the other in Africa."

Astounded, Becky said, "Africa?"

He shook his head up and down silently, the humor in his eyes like sun after rain. "You're thinking Ebola and witch doctors, right?"

"Well," Becky hesitated.

"Let me assure you, Julie lives in comfort. She's a surgeon in a big city hospital."

"Really? In Africa?"

"Oh, yes."

And so their conversation ran on, easily comfortable, ending only when Rachel came to tell her they were leaving.

When Becky stood, Harold plucked at her sleeve, the desperation and loneliness in his touch like a brand on her conscience.

"If you would only visit occasionally, I would have something to look forward to," he said, his blue eyes as if they were underwater, swimming in tears.

"I will try."

"Please do. I'm in Room 116. Forgive me for being a burden, but I have no one. The staff is good to me, but they don't care about my life, my story. I want to tell you about the Amish friend I had during the war. Let me tell you my story."

On the way home, as the van wound its way around the country roads, unloading occupants at homes and farms dotting the snow-covered land around them, Becky was quiet. She gazed out the window at the dark woods that rose from the snowscape like walls, spiny, undulating thickets of trees that gave her an unexplained sense of loneliness, as if the sight of those dark trees touched an emptiness within herself.

She tried to appear in a holiday mood, to banter and giggle, but she let it go after a time, knowing her heart was not in it. She thought only about the elderly people, the longing and desperation in Harold's plea. She had not told him her name. And who was Aretha Franklin? That was a nice name, Aretha. She'd never heard it before. She'd have to ask Mam if she could visit. Or Dat. Perhaps they would think it improper and refuse to let her go.

Why had she been so taken by these people? She felt as if she had stepped in a hole, slid down a long chute, and landed smack in the middle of a whole new world, one she had never imagined. She had known of "old people's homes" or "homes," the word that made every middle-aged Amish person shudder, roll their eyes, and renew their own inward conviction that none of their relatives would ever suffer the indignation of being "put away."

The Amish *fasark* their elderly. It was expected, required, and accepted.

CHAPTER 5

AND YET, AS SHE BRUSHED HER TEETH, DONNED her pajamas, and crawled into bed, shivering as she pulled up the heavy quilt, images of elderly Amish moved through her mind. She heard plenty, reading in the kitchen on the recliner the way she did.

Dat's parents—Elam and Sarah Esh—were in their late eighties. Back in Lancaster, his eight siblings had to take turns now, sleeping in their parents' home at night. Elam had had a stroke, which rendered the one side of his body almost useless. During the day he was in a wheelchair. His wife, a companion of sixty-one years, did what she could for him, feeding him the foods that were too messy for him to get to his mouth with his left hand, and helping him to the bathroom. But to bathe and dress him, and get him into his bed in the evening and out of it in the morning, required a stronger, younger person.

Elam and Sarah lived in a *daudyhaus*, the small house *uf da hof* attached to the rambling old farmhouse of their daughter Salome, married to Henry King, and their large family. The children were accustomed to helping *s' Daudys*. The arrangement worked well and everyone got along just fine until Daudy had a stroke.

At first when he came home from the hospital, Salome and Henry took over the *fasarking* of Daudy. They bathed him and fed him, balanced the checkbook, paid the bills, changed the propane tank in the cabinet of the gas lamp, did all the laundry when Mommy fell on the slippery *Kesslehaus* floor, cooked their meals, did the cleaning, and brought in the mail and the phone messages.

All the siblings came to visit. Everyone came regularly. They offered their assistance, wrote checks and hid them under the sugar bowl, then went home to their own busy lives, filled with children and jobs and community responsibilities.

Little by little, these extra duties wore Salome down. Like water on rocks, it rounded all her sharp corners, took away her spunkiness, and made her compliant. She was tumbled along by the demands of her ailing parents until she became weary, and bitterness sprouted like moss all over her. It was becoming too much.

Mam would come in from the phone shanty, her mouth compressed, shaking her head as she launched into yet another vivid account of *da Enos sei schveshta Mary* and what was wrong with her, not even offering to take her turn because she went to market. Well, which was more important, Mam would like to know, that market in Crompton or her own parents who were not long for this world, you mark my words, Nancy. Money was all that woman cared about, never mind what Enos said. Salome wouldn't be able to take it *mitt die zeit*, that was all there was to it. But Mam guessed that if everyone was too dense to see what this was doing to Salome, then they'd sit up and take notice once she was hauled off to Green Pastures, Nancy, you mark my words.

Mam's self-righteous ramblings rained from the ceiling, destroying Becky's concentration as effectively as Fourth of July fireworks. She marveled at her mother's ability to judge Mary so harshly, especially when she and Dat were too far away to help. She was amazed, too, at how efficiently she drew Nancy into the conversation and erased Becky as if she had been drawn on a chalkboard. One swift swab with the wet rag of her high opinion of Nancy, and Becky had disappeared from her mother's mind. You mark my words, Nancy.

But it was Becky who marked her words. She not only marked them. She filed them away in the cabinet that was her bright mind, storing them efficiently so she could take them out and examine them from time to time.

Then a letter came from Mary. Mam's head moved from side to side, her fingers gripped the white tablet paper, her lips moved in concentration, and she clucked as she read.

Her shoulders drooped, she sighed, then got herself a cup of coffee and began to talk—to Nancy.

Mommy had shingles. She was sure the painful virus that produced that terrible rash came from stress. Salome wasn't always nice to Mommy, especially when it came to the wash. Mommy wanted to do her own wash while she still could.

Salome thought she wasn't fit. She'd pinched her finger until it bled in the wringer, left the diesel engine running until the air compressor released the valve, then fell on the slippery floor.

Mommy fought valiantly for her rights. She was small and thin, with skin like parchment paper, but when her voice took on that hard quality and her words were thrown like painful pebbles, Salome did not flinch.

"Mommy, *du bisht net fit.*"

So Mommy pouted. She didn't help hull peas in June, which she loved to do. It took all her willpower to stay in her own house and not join the happy, talkative pea-hullers on the shady front porch, drinking tea and eating pretzels and raw peas. Forgiveness would come, but Salome needed to know that she was not pleased.

Mam clucked to Nancy. "That must be awful hard on Mommy. There stands her wringer washer and the double tubs. You know how she rinses her wash twice, once in Downy and once in vinegar. You know how white her whites are. And Salome is a slop with the wash. I'm sorry, Nancy, but she is. I never saw the likes. She's too much in a hurry to change water, so she washes the colored clothes first, and it's simply *hesslich* how the men's white socks look. I folded her wash already, and those men's socks are stiff and gray. You can't fold them the way I do, they're too stiff. I can't imagine what Mommy has to give up, letting Salome do her wash. She could still do it."

Behind her book, Becky thought her thoughts. She couldn't see Mam having the added responsibility of an aging person, who was not very strong or capable, doing laundry close by. She'd be a nervous wreck. Why she barely ever let Becky drive the pony, and certainly never let her walk alone to the river. But Becky said nothing.

Nancy did. In fact, Mam and Nancy became quite huffy about the way Mommy was being treated, whereupon Mam sat down and wrote Mary a letter, saying Salome had no right taking away Mommy's right to wash. Now with English people taking the keys to their aging parent's car, that was entirely different—there were other lives involved. But no one was going to get hurt allowing Mommy to wash with a wringer washer.

So Mary rode her scooter over to Salome, threw it in the front yard, and had a talk with her. She felt

Salome should allow Mommy to do her own wash, never saying a word about Sadie's letter. Better she doesn't know, she thought.

Salome kept her eyes downcast, made a heroic effort and swallowed the quick retort that rose to her lips, nodded her head, and agreed. All right, she said, all right. If that's how you feel. It must have helped that she had prayed fervently just that morning, *please, Lord, help me to be kind and considerate this day.*

She smiled a small smile, afraid to smile too widely lest she appear outwardly the way she felt inwardly— like the smiling wolf in the Little Red Riding Hood story. Ah, the tempest that rages within us all, she thought.

So Mommy did her wash. Her shingles got better, everyone took their turn at night the way they were supposed to, and the months went by.

Then Daudy was afflicted with bedsores. Half the family favored natural home remedies. "Keep him out of the hospital. Costs are high."

The other half thought he needed medical attention and hauled him off to the family doctor, who put him on antibiotics for infection, which displeased the other half immensely. But they gave themselves up in the Amish way of seeking to yield to the other—relinquishing your own way for someone else's—which, they all knew through *errforing*, is easier said than done.

Especially when it came to antibiotics.

"Awful unhealthy."

"Kills everything, even the good bacteria."

"Give him probiotics at noon," they said.

Salome said she would, and forgot.

When Abner came to take his turn that evening, Daudy complained of a dreadful stomachache. When Salome was asked about the probiotic, she threw her hands in the air and apologized. Abner lowered his eyebrows and told his sister they were extremely important, and not to let it happen again.

That was when Henry found his wife in the bedroom, curled in a fetal position, soaked Kleenexes in her hand, moaning softly as she cried. He became alarmed, took her in his strong arms, and murmured endearing words. He stepped up his share of caring for Daudy, and things went smoothly for a while longer, Salome's strength shored up by the sturdy pillars of her husband's love and admiration.

All of this went through sixteen-year-old Becky's head as she lay beneath the cozy quilts in her flannel pajamas on a cold night during the Christmas season. Here at Round Oaks she had witnessed the English way. English people, for one thing, had only two or three children, whereas the plain folks mostly had a whole pile. So Amish families had more help. They would never put their parents or siblings in a nursing home. It simply was not their way, which was an admirable trait.

Or was supposed to be. And was. Much of the time.

But as in all things where people are involved, it had its ups and downs, its good and, yes, bad. If you leveled everything out in Dat's family of Eshes, Salome definitely had way more than her share. If you put everything on a hanging scale, Salome's responsibility was so heavy, her side would sink straight to the bottom.

So what alternative did English people have in a situation such as Harold's? None. Not with having only two girls living thousands of miles away, his wife gone, and Harold unable to care for himself.

Yes, he was lonely, but he was also being taken care of. He paid to be there. And the caregivers were being paid, so he was not a burden to anyone. He was part of their job. He was part of the means by which they made money.

He had rights, so if things went awry, he could complain. And did, likely.

But there poor Daudy sat on his bedsores, without the normal sensation of pain he had prior to his stroke, and afraid to be a bother to his children. He probably wasn't as lonely as Harold, but a form of shame covered him like a net, and he floundered in it like a trapped fish.

Daudy had been strong, efficient in all his work, never been beholden to anyone. He hadn't planned on spending his golden years needing help to do almost everything, with one useless side of his body attached like the wrong piece of a jigsaw puzzle.

Pity for her grandfather welled up in Becky, causing pain that was almost physical. She wasn't that close to him, especially now that she lived so far away in Wisconsin and saw him once a year or less, but he was Dat's own father and had been as strong and as capable in his time.

So here was the thing. She couldn't do anything for Daudy except send him a card and write to him, which she did quite regularly. But she could visit Harold and other aging patients at Round Oaks.

Suddenly she was wide awake. She flipped on her back and opened her eyes wide, staring at the darkened ceiling. She could get a job at Round Oaks! She could help all those dear lonely souls, giving them their pills, singing to them, reading to them. She could learn how to change sheets and bathe them.

She wondered if she had to take a course and if her parents would allow this. She would ask. Definitely she would bring up the subject at the breakfast table and hope for the best.

It took her a long time to get to sleep, thinking of all the possibilities, the wonder of having a real job she would be so passionate about. This was not merely working for someone to make money; this felt more like a calling, something she could do that made her happy just thinking about it.

To her parents' credit, they listened. Fairly. They did
not break in while she was talking; they did not make
fun of her or become impatient. Becky blushed to tell
them that Harold said she had a nice voice (she didn't
mention Aretha Franklin) and that he wanted her to
visit, but she thought working there would be perfect.

"You need your GED to work at a place like that,"
Nancy said, drily, her eyebrows raised.

"Then I'll do it. You can do it by mail."

"No, you can't. It's all online these days," Nancy
said, sure of herself from her pedestal and squashing
Becky's dream with her superiority.

"Then I'll use the neighbor's computer. I'll do it."

Dat and Mam shook their heads from side to side
at the same time.

"No," Dat said.

"Huh uh," Mam said.

"You wouldn't know the first thing about it,"
Nancy said.

"I could learn."

"You are not allowed to go online to earn your
GED. Not on a computer, and certainly not at a
neighbor's house. You may, of course, visit this old

fellow, but as far as getting a job, I believe that is out of the question." Dat as usual spoke kindly, building the fence of discipline around his daughter with love. Becky knew she would not resist.

She did talk to Jake and Junior about it and said she was going to get a 12-volt battery, an inverter, and a computer. They hooted and roared with laughter, saying you needed a lot more than that to operate one—some kind of line or something from the phone company.

Becky threw a grooming brush at them, then swept the concrete floor of the horse barn and cried. She blubbered and hiccupped and sniffed. She lifted the corner of her apron to her nose and blew. That was gross, but there was no one to see.

She dried her face, marched solidly into the house, cut two slices of homemade bread, got down a pan, and slammed it on the burner. She toasted the butter-covered bread, spread it with peanut butter and strawberry jelly, put it on a plate, and took it to her room, along with two hard pretzels and three slices of white American cheese. She decided enough is enough. She'd get even with that Jake and Junior. Meanies. She wasn't done yet.

Christmas came.

On the evening of the twenty-fourth, which was their time to exchange gifts, Dat and Mam were both in a festive mood, handing out packages, smiling, and receiving gifts from the six children. A general chaos filled the well lit living room.

They enjoyed the gifts, ate cookies, candy, snack mix, and tangerines, sang Christmas carols, and held long and varied conversations. It was a time of closeness, a time of cheer and good wishes among all the children. Becky had even let go of her anger at Jake and Junior, choosing instead to walk around with her nose in the air, ignoring them completely, which seemed to work pretty well.

And then it was off to the Christmas singing.

Dat and Mam chose to stay home, Mam explaining that her headache was threatening to turn into a migraine because she had a lot to do before the twenty-seventh. That's when Dat's family would be visiting from Lancaster, close to fifty people arriving on a chartered bus.

The driveway leading to the Aaron Stoltzfus farm was alive with lights, strings of them—double yellow or silver headlights from the buggies that wound their way in the lane to the singing. The Christmas Eve singing was always special, like a giant open house. Everyone from miles around was invited—parents, grandparents, youth, school-aged children, toddlers, and babies. The singing of the German Christmas hymns they all loved so much rose steadily in volume as more and more folks arrived.

Becky was glad to see her friends but was surprised to find herself alone in the shop after Rachel Ann and Betty ran off, giggling between themselves. They hadn't bothered asking her to accompany them, so Becky shrugged her shoulders and sat on a tool bench, hoisting herself up with the aid of an overturned five-gallon bucket.

She was startled to see the lanky form of Daniel meandering across the shop, walking as if he had all night to reach his destination and not concerned whether he got there then. She groaned inwardly, wishing he'd go away. His small, light-colored eyes lit up as he approached.

"Merry Christmas, Becky!"

"Thank you. Merry Christmas to you, too."

"Daniel."

"Oh, yes, Daniel." She laughed in spite of her annoyance.

Without hesitation, blushing, or any sign of shyness, he said flatly, "Your voice is amazing. Do you mind if I sit close to you at every singing from now on?"

"Well, no, I guess not."

"Good. I'm going to then." His face was almost level with hers, seated high up on the tool bench the way she was, so when he smiled at her, she smiled back.

He sighed, leaned his elbows on the tool bench, and watched the knot of boys grow bigger. Turning his head, he looked at Rachel Ann and Betty as they ran past, squealing like newborn piggies.

"That should get someone's attention," he said, drily.

Becky snorted. "They hope."

"Why aren't you with them?"

"They ran off. I can't keep up. Besides, they don't really want me. My close friend and cousin is dating now, so I sort of got pushed onto them."

Daniel nodded but remained quiet.

"You just turned sixteen, right?"

"A couple months ago."

"You seem older."

"Do I?"

"Yeah."

The conversation turned to the evening singing at Round Oaks, and Becky found herself telling Daniel the whole story of Harold Epstein, about the loneliness in his eyes, her own grandparents, and the differences in their care.

He listened, nodded, watched her face, and nodded again, speaking a greeting to others as they walked by, but mostly he listened to her observations about life. When she finished, she felt a flush of humility creep across her face, figuring he'd think her stupid. Either way, she didn't care. It had helped to talk about it.

Finally, he said, "You might not need your high school diploma. I'd think that would be up to the administration at Round Oaks. Unless all these homes have a basic set of rules. I don't know. It might be worth a try to ask if they'd consider hiring you."

"You think?"

"I dunno. Might."

She almost said, "Go with me," but caught herself. She didn't even like him, so why would she ask him to accompany her on a mission that was so important? Nothing fazed this guy, that was the thing. It seemed he viewed the world through those unblinking, calm eyes and didn't get riled about anything.

"It could be worth a try," she agreed.

Jake stuck his head in a side door. "Becky. I'm leaving. If you want a ride, come on."

"Okay, I'm coming."

She leaned over to pick up her coat, accidentally brushing Daniel's shoulder with her arm. "Sorry."

"It's okay."

He stood directly in front of her, looked into her eyes, then down to the five-gallon bucket. "How'd you get up there?"

She nodded toward the bucket.

He kicked it away, his eyes creased by his smile. "Now you have to stay up there. Jake will leave without you."

"Put the bucket back. Give it here. Put it back." Becky felt the irritation. He was about as annoying as a clogged drain. She wished she could hit him with a plunger.

"I'll help you down."

"No!" Becky meant it. She was far too heavy. There was no way he could lift her down like a child, and there was no way she would allow him the chance to try. What a helpless predicament!

"Stop it. Give me that bucket."

He smiled, a slow, relaxed smile. "I'll tell you what. I'll give you the bucket if you'll ride home with me. I'm going to Levi Lantze's overnight—for Christmas dinner tomorrow—so I'll drop you right off. I bet Jake has a load, with Junior and those other guys."

Becky's head spun. Jake and Junior did not have anyone else to take home. They never did. Who in the world was this person standing here? He didn't want her to accompany him for the same reason guys asked to take girls home—to start a special friendship. She had just turned sixteen. She was too young.

Likely he was only being kind, as in genuinely looking out for her. He didn't want her in the way other guys asked the popular, thin girls if they could take them home. But what if he did?

Her thoughts spun, making no sense. She had never imagined this situation, and certainly not this soon. She was fat, not a girl anyone would consider. What did he mean by all this?

Red shirt, black vest, and neatly pressed trousers. Longish brown hair, small eyes, longish face but not ugly. In fact, the longer he stood there, the better he looked, as far as his facial features went. He had a nice, wide mouth and a pretty big nose, but not horribly, unnaturally big. Becky felt the thudding of her heart.

He looked as if he had no intention of putting the bucket over for her to step on. In fact, he didn't look as if he had any memory of a bucket having been there in the first place. He merely slid two big hands around her wide, soft waist, planted his feet firmly, and lifted her down before she had a chance to catch her breath.

"You're not so heavy," was all he said. "Now can I give you a ride home?"

She looked up at him. He was so tall and she was so short. She felt very much like a child.

Why did she say yes? Her biggest fear was sitting in a buggy with a potential suitor. She was so wide. She took up so much of the seat. It was too awful to think about. He couldn't even drive, stuffed against the door the way he would be.

But to be seated with Daniel was like finding the corner piece of a jigsaw puzzle. Everything fell into place. She never thought of her size. She was happy to be seated in a young man's buggy. This was the first time she was taken home by anyone, and she had only turned sixteen.

He was quiet, relaxed, funny, and easy to talk to. He made his intentions very clear in the best way possible, saying he hoped she knew that he wanted to begin a friendship as soon as she was ready, if she would consider doing that with him.

He slid a long arm around her shoulders and pulled her very slightly against him as he talked, then let her go. He said he never forgot the first sight of her, that she was made perfectly his size. Becky never remembered how she got down off that buggy or walked into the house.

CHAPTER 6

AFTER THE CHRISTMAS SINGING, MAM FELL into a fit of cleaning, cooking, and pudding-making, the likes of which Becky had never seen. *What in the world*, she thought, watching her mother's face turn red as a stop sign, sweat trickling from her forehead like a squeezed sponge, as she yelled at Nancy to turn down the draught on that woodstove, it didn't need to be ninety degrees in this kitchen.

Becky mostly stayed out of her way, taking her time cleaning the upstairs, grabbing a few moments to read a page of her favorite book. Anything to stay out of Mam's way. She guessed fifty-some people was quite a herd of relatives, coupled with all the letter-writing and phone messages about Mommy, and the tension between Mary and Salome and Mam herself.

Becky had her own opinions about Mam sticking her nose clear into Pennsylvania from way out here in Wisconsin, since she would not be able to help with Daudy's care. Why not keep her opinions to herself?

As usual, Becky shrugged her shoulders and did just that.

Even if she chose to air them, they'd be batted down like a swarm of hungry houseflies with the fly swatter, wielded by either Mam or Nancy.

The thing was, if Salome took on 95 percent of the responsibility for Daudy's care, then she was the one who should be allowed to make most of the decisions. She and Henry. Why did she have to concede so many of her opinions to Mary, who was wheeled off to market half the time, or—and this really irked Becky—to Mam and her high-mindedness, who lived hundreds of miles away and was unable to contribute any time?

She doubted whether Mam was too generous with the checkbook either, storing away all that Princess House stuff for Nancy, and Nancy unable to snare Allen the way she was.

Life was interesting. Her own life would have to be put on the back burner until all these holiday festivities were past, that was sure.

She bent down to use the handheld brush to scoop up the dust and dirt she had swept from each room, emptied the accumulation into the trash bag she held, then turned to begin cleaning the bathroom, a major chore with those big boys.

They were all slobs, every one of them. They left washrags lying in the bottom of the bathtub or slung across a faucet or scrunched on the shelf of the tub wall. Flying slathers of their bodywash stuck in blue blobs on the side of the bathtub. The blue rug was always wet, the washbasin never rinsed clean. Their towels lay on the floor, or, worse yet, were slung haphazardly across the shower curtain rod.

Today was no different. What a mess! She found dirty socks in corners, shaving cream on the wall, toothbrushes and capless toothpaste, combs, mirrors, and deodorant left everywhere. It was a hodgepodge of men's items taking over the whole bathroom.

Things had to change. One medicine cabinet and one narrow cupboard were not enough to keep this bathroom organized. If she complained, no one took her seriously anyway, so this mess called for some drastic measures.

She marched straight up the attic stairs, the cold like a slap on her face. She forgot how frigid an attic could be. Shivering, she stepped carefully over boxes, past rows of plastic hangers and an old blue and green playpen, to find the white bookcase she was looking for. There it was, sure enough.

She lifted a corner. It was very heavy. Oh, well. She tugged it out from under the eaves, heaved it upright, and stood panting. Whew, that thing was a load. Well, she needed it in the bathroom, so somehow she was going to get it there. On its side would be best.

She considered going to the barn for Dat, then thought better of it. For one, he was as busy as Mam right before the company, and two, he probably wouldn't allow it, saying she could wait till after the holidays.

She needed to help the bathroom. Elam's Kate, who lived in the nicest house in Lancaster County, would be coming, carrying her airs like a crown on her head. So if they lived in a square, white-sided cracker box, with a wooden patio in need of stain the only thing saving it from complete ugliness, she could at least organize the bathroom.

She laid the ungainly bookcase on its side, bent over, and grasping it on both sides, gave it a mighty

heave. It moved a few feet. She repeated the maneu-
ver until she had edged it to the stairs.

She scratched her head, caught her breath, then
tilted the bookcase down the first few steps. She
tested the weight, quickly deciding she could handle
this, and then slid the heavy piece of furniture down
the attic steps, too fast and much too loud, clunking
it against the attic door with a bang.

She waited, holding her breath, but there was no
response from the kitchen. Likely the eggbeater was
whirring and Mam's ears were shut tight from the
pressure within. Becky smiled, the thought of steam
escaping from Mam's rather heavily lobed ears and
sounding like the teakettle when the water boiled.
She was at the boiling point, no doubt.

Becky jumped, hearing her name called forcefully.
She turned to find Mam and Nancy, their eyes large
and frightened in pale faces, indignant.

"What happened?"

"Nothing."

"What was that crash?"

"I just slid the bookcase down the stairs sort of
fast."

"What are you doing, sliding that heavy old book-case down from the attic right before *S' Grishtag essa?*" Mam's chest was heaving, and Nancy had her "How could you" look perfectly in place.

Becky decided it was time to voice an opinion, let it fall where it may, then pick up the pieces after the storm of disapproval was over. She told her mother and sister to just turn around, make a left, and go look at that bathroom. It was a disaster, and the reason was that no one ever had enough space for all their junk. Furthermore, no one cared, "including you two," meaning Mam and Nancy.

It ruffled quite a few feathers, as she expected. She was soundly scolded by her mother, sniffed at in the most condescending manner by Nancy, and had her sanity and good judgment questioned. But Becky stood, her arms folded across her stomach and her mouth set in a straight line that did not bode well for either one. In the end, their voices faded and they went back down the stairs to their pies and puddings, leaving Becky to her own devices.

She lugged the heavy bookcase through the bath-room door, heaving, maneuvering, and tugging it into an upright position. She clapped the dust off her hands and nodded to it. "There you are, sir, in all your glory," she told the bookcase.

She wiped it with Lysol, got down all the clean towels from the too small cupboard and folded them differently, then stacked them neatly on a shelf, adding a stack of washcloths. She pounded down the stairs to ask Mam for a turntable, got down a few mugs from the cupboard, and set about arranging everything in an orderly fashion. The turntable went into the cupboard. On it, she set the boys' toothpaste, shaving cream, soap, and all the extras that cluttered up so much of the minimal space the cupboard afforded.

She scrubbed and whirled, rinsed and scoured, finally collecting soaps from Nancy's room and her own. She put them in a clear, round vase, then stepped back to survey her work. Not bad.

If this was her bathroom, her very own, like after she was married, she would paint these walls a dusty aqua green, put up a white, poofy curtain and white trim, hang a pretty picture of the sea, and add a bunch of other white sea stuff. She didn't really know what all that would be. She had never been to the sea or ocean or beach, whatever you wanted to call it. Maybe "vacation." Elam's Kate went every year. Lucky girl.

Well, we're Wisconsin hicks, so we'll just be who we are. That thought brought contentment back to Becky, who was glad to live here on the farm in the cold and the snow and the beauty of the extended Christmas season. She was happy to have the Christmas dinner, grateful for all the relatives who would rain down upon them tomorrow.

She had a feeling that some of the relatives would cause a much greater impact than a raindrop. In fact, they would be more like an entire bucket of water dumped on Mam.

Going to her room, Becky picked up her journal, ripped out a few pages, and with a fine-lined black marker, made signs for the newly cleaned and organized bathroom.

"Wring washcloth. Hang over side of tub."

"Rinse basin after brushing."

"Pick up all dirty socks. Sock monster will bite."

"Put towels in hamper."

"All violators will be pushed down the stairs."

What a hooting and hollering when the boys found the bathroom completely rearranged, with written instructions and threats! They knew it was Becky and teased her unmercifully. Becky loved it and reveled in all the attention. She told her brothers she was lurking in the hallway and would keep track of whoever went through those bathroom doors and who emerged. If they left it looking the way they had before, she was serious, she'd push them down the stairs.

She carried out her threats, or tried to, catching Abner knocking his toothbrush on the side of the basin and leaving smears of dark blue Colgate toothpaste all over the sides. When he emerged, she screeched, grabbed his arm, and pulled him toward the stairs. He resisted with great force, but Becky was powerful. With all that weight leaning against him, he soon realized he was actually in great danger of being pushed down the stairs.

In the end, they both burst into helpless fits of laughter and sat side by side on top of the steps as

Becky told him she was serious, things had to change in that bathroom.

Abner put an arm around her shoulder and squeezed affectionately. "Ah, Becky, you are the best little sister ever."

"Not so little, unfortunately."

Abner glanced at her, a grin lighting up his face. "Jake tells me someone thinks you're just the right size."

"What does he know?"

"Something, evidently."

"I'm much too young to be thinking of anything seriously."

Abner nodded. "That's why I like you so much, Becky. For a girl, your common sense is just amazing."

"For a girl?"

"Well, no insult intended. But you know what I mean."

Becky nodded, completely at ease. Among her people, women and girls had their place, which in many ways was a step below the menfolk in their lives. The men were respected as leaders, the women as helpmeets and not leaders or decision-makers, at least publicly and formally. It was just a matter of being raised that way, even if the women sometimes stepped out of their role as lesser vessels, causing a discordant note in the mellow music of God's plan!

And so the bus arrived, plowing its way through the falling snow. So large and formidable, the bus was like a barn on wheels, rolling in the lane powerfully and steadily, as if the snow was a minor annoyance. It disgorged relatives in a constant, black-clad stream of hats and coats, punctuated by brightly wrapped Christmas gifts, suitcases, and diaper bags, squalling babies and carsick children, who were pale and un-happy. Their mothers carried Cool Whip containers filled with the poor toddlers' breakfasts that had not been in their stomachs very long at all.

These children were not used to traveling in fast-moving vehicles. Only occasionally were they allowed to ride along to town in a car or van. Even then, some mothers sat beside their children, nervously fingering a plastic container, watching a little face lose its color as the driver swung around another turn in a hurry to get to Walmart. He knew the wait would be lengthy, so the quicker he got there, the better.

Young mothers knew exactly which drivers were notorious for speeding around curves and across hills, causing their children's stomachs to clench with nausea. Chiropractors, Dramamine, holding a lemon— the cures were endless, but in the end, it was simply easier to leave toddlers at home whenever possible.

Mam stood on the porch, a beacon of welcome, blinking back tears as she shook hands, exclaimed at the growth of the children, and expressed the gladness she felt to *mol vidda eich sayna.*

Dat greeted everyone at the door of the bus, his black hat steadily decorated by the falling white snowflakes, the shoulders of his black coat turning to gray lace as he pumped hands and patted shoulders. It was just so good to see everyone *mol vidda.*

Nancy and Becky, dressed in their holiday red, welcomed relatives in the kitchen, directed them to the bathrooms, held babies they had never seen, and squealed in delight as their cousins, Kate, Laura, Emma Mae, Mary, and Hannah, fell upon them like colorful tropical birds, as brilliant and as noisy.

Oh, it was so good to be with family. Until Mam discovered that Mommy stayed home with Daudy. Her eyes filled with tears as both hands went to her mouth.

"But why? Why did you leave her at home?"

A gray fog of disharmony settled around the adults, chasing the gladness effectively into the corners of the room as everyone sensed how clearly upset Mam was. Voices chimed together, the reasons thick and plentiful.

"She wouldn't leave Daudy."

"She couldn't travel all this way."

"She didn't want to go."

Mam's lips pursed. "She just wrote me a letter. I just got it this week. She looked forward to being here so much."

Going to the wooden letter holder on the wall, she retrieved a white envelope, extracted a single sheet of lined paper, unfolded it, and searched for the sentence Mommy had written. "Here it is. 'We are looking forward to seeing all of you on the twenty-seventh.'"

Mam lifted her eyes, large and accusing, searching each relative's face, a judge in black robes with only a sliver of mercy available.

Dat scratched the side of his face, a gesture he used when he became uncomfortable. "So what did happen that Mommy stayed home? You know that this could very well be the last time she sees her own son and his family."

Henry spoke for all of them, his voice level with kindness. "She really wanted to come, I believe. She looked forward to it, just the way she wrote. But when it came right down to it, it seemed she just couldn't do it. She couldn't leave Dat."

His eyes found and held Mam's accusing gaze, the kindness and truth in them easily wrestling down the accusing glare he found there.

The fog was banished by Henry's goodwill, the wave of Christmas cheer was summoned from the corners of the room, and the festivities began.

Mam was the center on which the wheel of the Christmas dinner turned. Red faced, with eyes snapping, she called out orders. Some sisters-in-law stood at the sink in clouds of steam, wielding potato mashers, their shoulders' rhythm to the arm-plunging movements like a song, a cadence. They laughed and talked, then stepped back to wipe their steaming glasses and to let someone else have a turn.

Mam moved to the stove, flung the oven door open, and proudly lifted out the champion of all dishes, the Christmas *roasht*. The oversized blue agate roaster was steaming hot. Using heavy hot pads, she set it on the countertop, removed the lid with a flourish, and stepped back smiling, beaming proudly.

No contest here. Mam made the best *roasht*. The very best. Her secret was chunks of chicken, baked and cubed to perfection. She cut the celery in fair-sized chunks as well, and did not broil all of it in butter. She like to mix some in raw to give a better celery flavor.

She kept the bread cubes oversized, too, mixing them with lots of butter and gently seasoning them with only salt and pepper. She stirred everything together lightly with a careful hand, adding the beaten eggs last. Yes, there was a secret to outstanding *roasht*. Absolutely.

The gravy was thick and golden, rich with good chicken fat and a dash of ginger ale added as a stabilizer, although it was a bit salty.

The potatoes were mashed with butter and cream cheese. The peas were from the garden's abundance, early peas, picked when they tasted like ambrosia. *Gute arpsa*, they all said.

The noodles were homemade, thick and flecked with browned butter. The *Kaltgraut* was fresh, the cabbage having been grated that morning, then seasoned with vinegar, sugar, and salt.

Hard-boiled eggs were drowning in pungent, pickled, red-beet juice. They were eaten cut in half and salted by each individual.

Mam had picked the little green pickles each morning they were in season to make sure she got the smallest and the youngest cucumbers. She carefully washed them, cut their ends off, and brined them for seven days.

These were her seven-day sweet pickles. She made them every year, feeling mildly superior to those lazy housewives who let their cucumbers grow to the size of a zucchini squash, claiming that banana pickles were their family's favorite, those limp, yellow, peeled oddities that were drowned in sugar and turmeric. They were disgusting, in Mam's culinary opinions, which were numerous and well flaunted.

After that came the desserts. A train of cakes, pies, and puddings, followed by fruit and Jell-O, the caboose aimed at those who had a conscience about healthy eating. The walnut layer cake had caramel icing. Mam's chocolate cake was always the men's favorite. Along with pecan pie, pumpkin pie, and lemon meringue.

There was always Christmas salad, with its ribbons of red, green, and white Jell-O. Next to it was date pudding and butterscotch tapioca. And of course, the necessary bowl of fruit salad, made with canned peaches and pears, fresh grapes, oranges, and bananas. Some younger women added kiwis and strawberries, but Mam said those grainy, slippery kiwis ruined good, traditional, Amish fruit salad.

Everyone ate and ate, bantering across the tables, spirits high as stomachs were filled with the Christmas feast.

They hand-washed all those dishes, and everyone eventually found a seat, circling around the sprawling kitchen and spilling into adjoining rooms. The children grew impatient and fidgety, knowing that the singing would go on and on and on, before the gifts were allowed to be distributed.

Becky sang along with the cousins, trying hard to sing quietly so as not to draw attention to herself, too aware of the compliments she had received this season. It wouldn't do to stand out too much or to seem to be showing off.

Presents were distributed afterward, much to the delight of the little ones. Only then did the visiting begin in earnest, the women pairing off into groups of two or more, Mam eager to hear all the latest news from her home.

Salome sat apart, her arms crossed, her face pale and drawn, a child on her lap as she peeled a tangerine. Becky felt a stab of pity and so broke apart from her gaggle of hysterical cousins and sat down beside her aunt. She talked easily about the old people at Round Oaks, and how she'd love to have a job working with the elderly and feeble.

Suddenly Salome leaned close and put a hand on her wide knee. "Oh, Becky," she breathed. "Why don't you come home with us and care for Daudy and

Mommy? You would be an answer to our prayers. An angel of mercy."

She glanced around the kitchen furtively, then lowered her voice to a whisper. "I can hardly take it anymore."

Pools of tears gathered in Salome's gentle eyes. She blinked furiously to rid herself of the unwelcome display of what she viewed to be self-pity and weakness.

"Just come, Becky. I'm serious. If you feel you have a fondness for these old people, then definitely, you should do it."

Becky stammered. "But I meant a job. Making money, you know? You couldn't afford to pay me. And besides, I've heard quite enough of all the *ch-vistats'* opinions and helpful advice. How could I ever please everyone?"

Salome lowered her hand, dabbing at her eyes. "You couldn't. I can't."

"Should families be this way, Salome? I mean, Mam gets so upset and marches to the phone. Since I was at Round Oaks, all of this has given me much to think about."

"You mean . . . ?"

"Well, frankly, Salome, we would never put away our old people the way English people do. But our way isn't exactly an oasis of love either."

Salome looked at her sharply. "We are only human. We do the best we can." Her tone was clipped, hard as a handful of pebbles flung in her face.

"Oh, I know. I know." Quickly, Becky tried to rectify her mistake.

She drifted away from Salome after that, having quickly changed the subject to a lighter note.

All afternoon she listened to the foolish prattling of her Lancaster cousins and became quite the life of the conversation herself with her quick wit and dry sense of humor. But her mind was elsewhere.

Could she leave Wisconsin? Did she want to set herself smack in the middle of that hornet's nest of ill feelings where the care of Daudy was concerned? Could she care lovingly for the grandfather she barely knew, for a distant grandmother who seemed as alien as Harold Epstein?

She approached her mother, catching her in the pantry, and told her quickly what Salome had said.

Mam's eyes sought Becky's face. "Oh, Becky, you don't want to do that."

"Why not?"

"I thought you were going to try for a job here."

"I can't without my GED."

Mam gave Becky a push. "We must get back to our company. Just forget about your idea."

So Becky did. She took her mother's advice and went back to the frivolity of her cousins, enjoying the remainder of the day by tucking away the weighty matter of Salome's invitation.

When the bus returned, the family scrambled for their wraps. They stowed their presents neatly in boxes, filled jugs with ice water, and wrapped leftovers to be eaten on the way home.

Tears flowed and hugs were everywhere, after discovering that a handshake just wasn't adequate conveyance of love between individuals. Babies were pulled from sound naps, bundled into fleece blankets, and carried through the still falling snow.

"Good-bye!" Good-bye!"

"*Machts gut. Machts gut!*"

As the bus lumbered off through the gray, whirling evening, the family turned to go inside, relieved to know their guests were scheduled to stay at a Day's Inn about a hundred miles away. That was a huge comfort to Mam, with the snow coming down like it was and the interstates slick with slush.

"Oh, the salt and calcium trucks will be out like a swarm of bees," Dat said, then chuckled. "Wonder how many TVs will be turned on tonight?"

"Ach, Dat. Now."

Dat laughed again. "Maybe not Henry and Salome's, but I bet the rest won't sleep much."

Becky caught Mam's "tsk" of self-righteousness, but it was edged with love and mercy.

CHAPTER 7

AND SO THAT WINTER BECKY FACED SOME tough choices.

January was bitterly cold and filled with endless swirling, biting snow that drifted around the barn in tight piles. It required hours of hard shoveling just to keep the path to and from the house open.

Salome's needs tugged at her heart.

Soon after the family Christmas, Becky visited Harold Epstein in Room 116 at the Round Oaks facility. It was the first of many more visits. His voice shook as he took them both back to a gentler time when the world was a simpler place. Becky loved to sit at his side, listening to the gravelly voice unfold the years of his life. It seemed as if that alone was all he needed. A listening ear, a caring heart.

She would sing to him or read from his books of poetry or the Bible, passages he loved from Isaiah or the Psalms. Always he would beg her to stay only a bit longer, and always she would.

He asked the administrator if she could apply for a job, but was told firmly, that no, not without her GED. Company policy.

Harold was not happy about this at all and said he was going to speak to his daughters about moving.

Then they found the message on voicemail.

Salome had had a breakdown. A nervous breakdown. Her nerves were completely shattered.

Mam spent hours on the phone. She sat with Dat late at night, discussing the situation.

Evidently, Mommy had been showing signs of dementia before Christmas, which was behind Mam's confusion about her letter, followed by her refusal to come on the bus. Daudy's bedsores had worsened to the point that he was taken to the hospital for extensive care. Then Mommy boiled a jar of pickles, thinking she was heating green beans to eat with her supper of stewed crackers.

She blamed Salome for hiding Daudy from her on purpose, telling her she finally got her way after years of trying to get Daudy away from her.

This all happened when Henry went to New Jersey for a few days with a group of men to help rebuild from storm damage, leaving Salome with far too much on her shoulders. The neighbor lady who was to help proved to be unreliable, even hostile. So Salome sat on the couch and began to cry and couldn't stop.

Mary still went to market but helped more than she used to. Rachel took most of her parents' care on herself, but clearly, there was a huge need.

Becky told Mam she would go. She said the words with her mouth, but her heart was not in it. She didn't know her grandparents, and the Lancaster cousins seemed as annoying as children, the inconsistency of their silly lives as senseless as too thin vanilla pudding.

Becky had tried hard to fit in with them, but she just couldn't quite make it. What if she got all the way to Lancaster and remained an outsider, having to live with a mentally unstable Salome? What would she do with aunts hovering over her with their outsized magnifying glasses, scrutinizing every move she made, then discussing it endlessly among themselves like snappy little dogs chewing on rawhide bones?

She was, after all, doing her duty by visiting her aging old friend, Harold. She still liked the atmosphere at Round Oaks, loved being there and listening to the professional swishing of rubber-clad soles on carpeting, the smell of fresh coffee in the morning, the trundling of the laundry cart. She longed to work among them, still, but she'd admitted finally that it was impossible, that the administrator would not bend the rules.

Daniel wasn't really in her life, staying so aloof, until she wasn't sure at all that the Christmas evening conversation had happened. Had it just been a distant dream? Did she even want it to be real? She didn't know.

And she wasn't sure she could deal with an old grandparent who was slowly losing her mind.

When the cold loosened its grip so that the snow slid off metal roofs and began to form runnels of water through low snowbanks, Dat left the farm in the care of the boys, packed his bags, and went to see his parents on Amtrak.

Upon his arrival, he called home and left a message, telling his wife to come and bring Becky if she was still of a mind to come. Mam was terrified of the train, but Abner made all the arrangements, told Becky she was easily smart enough to travel with Mam, and sent them off.

Becky sat beside her mother and watched the white landscape rush past. She became really hungry and thirsty but felt too timid to say anything, her size always a displeasure on Mam's mind. Finally she asked Mam if she'd brought anything to eat. Mam reached into her purse and brought out a package of Lance peanut butter crackers, without a drink. So Becky ate the crackers and got more and more thirsty. But she sat in that train in complete misery rather than ask Mam for a drink.

Just when she thought she'd suffocate from a dry throat, Mam asked if she wanted to eat in the dining car where some of the other passengers were going. She nodded and followed her mother, trying to make herself as small as possible, yet feeling very much like an elephant trying to squeeze through a narrow hallway.

The reward was dinner. A good roast beef sandwich with gravy and French fries, a bowl of applesauce, and a slice of cherry pie that was so sour it puckered her mouth.

Mam laughed at her. She laughed at her when they tried to settle down for the night, too. Becky flipped and turned and sighed, trying to get decently comfortable, which she finally decided was an impossibility. She gave up and sat upright, sleeping with her head falling sideways, and waking up with such a stiff neck she was sure it would be for always.

When Becky told Mam she would walk on a forty-five degree angle from here on out, Mam laughed long and sort of loud, which came as a big surprise to Becky. She didn't think she was that funny.

Puzzled, she looked at her mother reclining in the seat beside her. She had laughed more on this train than she had for months at home. Maybe mothers just were that way   uptight and care-worn by the daily grind of washing and cleaning, cooking and sewing, spinning around them like the fibers of a cocoon, ensnaring and enslaving them without them being fully aware of it. Or not knowing what to do about it if they did understand the dilemma. Perhaps that was what pushed up their eyebrows and drew lines of tension around their mouths.

Life was different on the train, away from the daily grind of caring for those four boys who ate like horses and always needed new pants and shirts and lunches packed and thermoses filled. She might just be like a butterfly freed from its cocoon. Now she could sail along on the train, and for one day and night not worry about dishes and laundry and boys.

She asked Mam if she felt freed.

Mam laughed and said, "Ach, Becky, I like my life at home, the work, the daily duties. What else would I do? It's the way of the Amish woman, and I wouldn't want it any other way. It's a fulfilling life."

"Why don't you laugh at home, then?"

"I do."

"Hardly ever."

Mam looked at Becky, really looked at her, a twinkle in her eyes containing leftover humor. "Becky, I laugh at you a lot more than you know. I laugh at you especially when you get so mad. I know I shouldn't. That's why I look out the kitchen window and shake all over while tears run down my face. I'm laughing so hard. You are really funny sometimes.

"I don't know why I don't let myself laugh openly at you. Maybe it's just my upbringing. You know how we're taught that we shouldn't laugh too much at our children because it can make them *grosfeelich*."

"You think I'm *grosfeelich*?"

"Oh, my, no. Sometimes you are just very, very funny."

"Is that a compliment?"

"Yes, it is."

"Thank you."

"You're welcome."

Mam smiled at Becky, a smile that revealed admiration and a sense of pride that rose and fluttered around Becky's heart, filling a need she didn't know she had.

Mam sighed. "You know, Becky. I'm beginning to wonder if I don't hold Nancy a bit higher than I should. I do admire her, and, yes, I admit, it's fun having a girl in her *rumschpringa* years. But you are so easy, so uncomplicated. I should tell you this more often. I appreciate you just for being you."

Becky's throat tightened, the tip of her nose burned, and for one horrifying moment she was afraid she would cry.

"I'm too fat, Mam."

Mam placed a hand over Becky's. "Oh, Becky, don't say that. It sounds so harsh."

"You don't like it."

"I struggled to accept it as you approached young womanhood, yes. But you weren't aware of my feelings, I hope."

"Mam, now come on. It was written all over your face when you sewed for me."

Mam smiled. "Well." Then she said, "I'm sorry, Becky."

"Apology accepted."

Mam sighed. The train rumbled on, and Becky said, "You were never mean."

"No, I never was."

When the train pulled into the station in downtown Lancaster, Becky walked off the train carrying a treasure she never had before, the security of her mother's love. Their talk had come very close to being heart-to-heart, sufficient for her well-being by far.

They arrived *ons' Daudy Esha* on an afternoon in March, finding the landscape emerging from the snows of winter—brown fields, mud, patches of dirty snow fringed with gray, melting particles, traffic hissing and spattering on Route 340, shining black buggy wheels encrusted in mud the color of caramel corn.

"Too wet to plow," Dat said.

He paid the driver, got out, and helped Mam with her suitcase. Smiling at Becky, he told her to be prepared. "*S' Dat's sinn net goot.*"

Which proved to be an understatement. A dire one.

Becky had been with her grandparents only a handful of times in her life, but they were now almost beyond recognition.

Daudy sat in a hospital bed, cranked up as high as it would go, propped upright by pillows that appeared yellowed and rumpled. He smiled with only one part of his face. His speech was slurred, slow, and incomprehensible.

Dat and Mam walked to his side and gripped his hand, bending to hear what he had to say.

Becky hung back. The smell, for one thing, was overpowering. A strong, acidic odor of herbal tinctures, diapers, and what else? Her eyes took in the spots on the linoleum, the cup of warm water with a broken straw, the rain-splattered, fingerprinted windows that had not been washed in months.

When her grandmother appeared, it was like a dagger to her heart. Much too thin, the woman wore a dress that was filthy from too many days without a washing, her covering yellowed and crooked, her hair uncombed.

She said hello politely as if to strangers, then recovered and said, "Enos! Sadie!" Clearly delighted, she welcomed them warmly, then turned to Becky, puzzled. She asked her son who the *fett maedle* was, then turned and shook hands with her formally when Dat told her it was "our Becky."

Becky smiled and greeted her grandmother, hiding the despair that clung to her with a viselike grip. She couldn't stay here by herself. Mam and Dat would leave, and she would be here in this depressing *daudyhaus* without the slightest clue about how to proceed. For a moment, she panicked, losing all sense of direction.

She had a good while to take stock of the situation, however, when her parents went to confer with the remainder of the family. Salome was doing better, but she could not be saddled with the responsibility of her aging parents. Her nerves would not take it.

Becky looked through the cupboards, found a frying pan and a saucepan, then heated tomato soup and fried a few beef patties. She opened a jar of pickles and placed a bowl of applesauce on the table.

She filled a Melmac soup bowl with the steaming tomato soup, crumpled in a handful of saltines and a dollop of applesauce, and told Mommy to eat. Like a child, she showed her delight, promptly lifting a spoonful of soup to her trembling, birdlike mouth.

Becky was surprised by, then frightened of, the hunger in her grandfather's eyes. He was starving. She went to the drawer in the cupboard, found a tablespoon, then began ladeling the hot soup into his mouth as fast as she could, wiping off the excess with a paper towel. He devoured the one fried beef patty, raised his hand, and pointed for another.

Something inside Becky stirred. She felt fiercely protective of this aging, neglected couple who were her own flesh and blood.

Her grandmother went to the pantry and retrieved a cake pan, slid back the lid, and presented a perfectly baked shoofly cake. Shaking her finger at Becky, she said, "They think I can't do this anymore. Ha. Look at this. It's perfect. What Rachel and Mary don't know won't hurt them." Giggling, she sat down and helped herself to a generous slice. Becky laughed with her, then cut a chunk for Daudy.

She heard a garbled, "*Vett millich. Millich. Vett millich.*"

Quickly, Becky went to the refrigerator, found a glass container of milk, and poured it over the shoofly cake. She fed it all to Daudy, wiped his face, then patted his arm.

The old face softened with appreciation, his garbled "*Denke*" a benediction.

She pulled up the sheet, cranked his bed lower, adjusted his pillows, and said he could rest awhile till she could get him ready for bed.

Mommy was already washing dishes when Becky helped herself to a steaming bowl of tomato soup and saltines.

Long into the night, she conferred with her parents. In the end, they went home to the farm in Wisconsin, leaving Becky to take over most of the responsibility for her grandparents.

Becky cried that first night, just like she cried before her sixteenth birthday. Then she squared her shoulders, took a deep, calming breath, and faced the situation head-on. No use whimpering and crying. She was here now. She had promised to do her best so she would.

She told herself this in firm tones, if a sort of panic in your thoughts can be called a tone. Her eyes were open, staring at the ceiling, the unaccustomed display of traffic lights like human-made northern lights keeping her awake.

The small room with the twin-sized bed was constantly changing from dark to a brilliant white or yellow as cars whizzed past. With each vehicle that stopped at the intersection, she heard the grinding of loose stones. In addition, there were loud bellows from pickup trucks and softer sounds from small cars, but each and every one was as annoying as the one before.

Her grandmother snored deeply, a steady rhythm of burbling sounds from her old nose. Or old throat or adenoids, whatever, Becky thought. A gruff duplicate of the same sound emanated from the hospital bed in the front room where her grandfather lay in a deep sleep.

She thought of all she would need to learn, grimacing at the thought of the old unwashed bodies, the grease and filth of her grandmother's dress front. They were so old. They had lived all their lives taking a hot bath only on Saturday evenings, wearing the same clothes for two or three days, maybe even longer. The odor in the house was the smell of unwashed bedclothes and laundry, plus dank towels that hung on their rack for weeks.

Daudy's hair needed a shampoo so desperately, but how did one go about washing hair if the person was bedfast? There had to be a way.

Well, she would do laundry first thing in the morning. She would find every sour-smelling item in the house and wash them all in steaming hot water and Tide with bleach in Mommy's wringer washer, then hang everything out to dry on the wheel line. She would bathe Daudy from head to toe, send Mommy to the bathtub, and deal with the dirty house.

In the morning, she woke to find Mommy puttering around the kitchen, wearing her flannel nightgown with a large safety pin at the neck. Strands of loose threads dangled from the hem like spiderwebs.

Quickly, Becky rose, took her suitcase to the bathroom, and washed and dressed before greeting her grandmother, who seemed delighted to see her. She called her Becky and told her she was making breakfast.

Becky decided to let her, but kept an eye on her as if she were a child. When she asked Salome to help with Daudy's sheets, she was met with a cold stare and a clipped, "It's not time to wash them."

Becky returned the look with one colder than Salome's and said in measured tones, "I'm taking care of

Daudy and Mommy, so I will say what gets washed and when."

Salome whimpered, "Now you're saying I'm sloppy."

Becky didn't answer as she turned on her heel. Salome followed her, making excuses about not being well. Becky wanted to feel the slightest twinge of sympathy but found none, so she didn't bother answering.

Salome said they didn't wash Daudy's hair. They used a product called Dry Shampoo. And Becky wouldn't need to bathe Daudy; that was Henry's job.

Becky's mind was grinding away, the gears lining up in perfect symmetry. Yes, she wanted a washbasin on the floor, another on the nightstand, and a pitcher of warm water for rinsing. She would need a towel. As she barked orders, Salome obeyed reluctantly. Mommy grimaced and wrung her hands as they gently tugged the upper half of Daudy off the bed and began scrubbing. When Becky was finished, Daudy was smiling, Salome was laughing, and Mommy was throwing her hands in the air and saying, "*Ach, du yay, du yay, dya fasaufet ihn noch!*"

Daudy raised one finger of his good hand and wag-
gled it at his wife.

Henry finished the bath. Becky brushed Daudy's
teeth and shaved him on the spots he couldn't reach.
They changed his bedding, plumped his pillows, and
fed him stewed crackers and dippy eggs with homemade ketchup and sausages. He swallowed his medi-
cation and vitamins obediently, sighed, and smiled
his lopsided smile. "*Denke*, Becky," he said.

When he fell asleep almost immediately, they were
afraid he had been through too much, being moved
from the bed like that.

Mommy was the biggest challenge. Salome's and
Henry's children drifted into her part of the house
like orphans with sticky mouths and wet muddy
shoes, making themselves at home without asking
permission, playing noisily on the floor with the old
tin box of Tinkertoys and empty, wooden spools.

Becky washed walls and windows and floors. She
sprayed degreaser on sticky green window blinds and
scoured the bathroom and each tiny bedroom.

Mommy slapped Becky's shoulder when she became upset as she watched her clean and defrost the

refrigerator. She said those peas would still be good, stewed with Ritz Crackers and milk. When Becky showed her the gray-green mold covering half the bowl, Mommy said you could scrape that off.

Becky waited till her back was turned or she became distracted, which was quite often, then swiftly emptied every little Pyrex container of moldy food, sour milk, curdled cheese, and yogurt piled high with gray fuzz. She dumped limp celery, slimy mashed potatoes, and old wrinkled tangerines dressed in their own fuzzy gray sweaters of mold.

They ate oatmeal for supper. Becky tumbled into bed with only part of the cleaning done. She cried from sheer weariness and homesickness, covered with an impending sense of gloom. To stay here would take all she had. She would have to tap into reserves of strength she didn't know if she possessed. She could only hope that she was strong enough to meet each new problem as it arose.

She prayed now, really prayed, sometimes begging God to help her through. No more absentminded *Miede Binnichs* for Becky. She acknowledged a Higher Power, an Almighty Hand above her, and felt guidance from a Presence she had been accustomed to hearing about all her life. Here in Pennsylvania, so many miles from her home in Wisconsin, God became real. She learned to pray, to draw on that source of power much higher than her own.

There were days when she couldn't stand the sight of weary, depressed Salome and her unkempt children. She was ashamed, even alarmed at her strong animosity toward an aunt who was doing the best she could. For Salome, who had weak nerves and was tied down with all her little ones, the sun hid behind a bank of black, scudding clouds called Depression.

It irked Becky over and over how she would sit on Daudy's couch, talking and letting those little ones run wild. They would pull down a plastic pot of African violets, spill juice and water, and ask for candy and crackers and pretzels, which Mommy stashed away on top of the refrigerator behind the cornflakes.

If Becky would not produce these treats for her children, Salome would get up, push the cornflakes aside, procure a bag of lollipops, and proceed to hand them out. That left Becky to wipe the floor, a cloud of steam enveloping her like a teakettle when Salome and her children finally took their leave.

Mommy always got upset when Salome did this, which was pitiful. In her state of dementia, it was very important to Mommy that the lollipops stayed hidden away behind the cornflakes. Sometimes she would cry like her heart was broken.

The day came when Becky held her in a soft, comforting hug, soothed her with the promise that she would buy more, then marched straight over to Henry's and confronted Salome while Henry was in the kitchen.

"This is what Becky said," Salome would repeatedly tell all the sisters, playing the poor damaged martyr to the hilt. "She said we have to stay home. If we can't care for Daudy, then 'don't sit over here in their space all afternoon and make it more difficult for me.' She said that. She's only sixteen, and she had the gall to say that to me."

The sisters sympathized accordingly, knowing Salome couldn't take much with her weak nerves. But the minute she left, they actually did some fist-pumping, agreeing that *Enosa Becky* was a gift, a godsend, a wonder.

Where did she get it, all that common sense in one so young? They nodded their heads in the end. Yes, Enos had been like that at sixteen.

CHAPTER 8

WHEN SPRING CAME, BECKY HAD A ROUTINE firmly established. She washed and cooked and cleaned, sewed dresses for herself in her spare time, and even joined a group of Lancaster County youth who called themselves the Hummingbirds.

She had a few good friends and met some interesting boys, but she wasn't attracted to anyone. No one asked her out either, which didn't surprise her. She knew boys weren't particularly attracted to girls her size, so that was fine.

Lancaster was a veritable metropolis, almost a New York City with its hustle and flow! Buggies drawn by spirited horses, cars and trucks, tractors and bikes, scooters and pedestrians, it never stopped. Even at night the dark was not really dark with twinkling lights in the distance. The English neighbors all had pole lights that flickered on at twilight like gigantic lightning bugs.

Becky wrote letters to her family and called Mam and Nancy, swallowing back tears of homesickness. Sometimes the desire to see Wisconsin got so strong she thought she couldn't stay in Lancaster one more week. But the homesickness always passed when she went back into the house and Daudy asked her to read from *Die Botschaft*, which she loved to do. Expressions of concern, humor, happiness, recognition, and love all passed over Daudy's face like changing weather as she read to him.

The broiling summer heat was hard on Daudy and Mommy. They both withered like lettuce left out on the counter, their breathing quick and shallow when they took their afternoon naps in the ninety-degree heat.

Henry set up a fan attached to a 12-volt battery, but Mommy didn't like it. She said it was noisy, and that they never had one of those when she was growing up. Daudy came down with a cold, a stiff neck, and a steady drip down the back of his throat. When he became nauseated and upset, he blamed the fan rigged up to that buggy "battry" and asked Henry to remove the fan and put the "battry" back in the buggy where it belonged.

Becky picked beans and canned them, cooking them for three hours in two agate canners. That operation turned the little house into a steaming sauna, which evidently bothered her grandparents less than the fan with its unaccustomed noise. She learned to can red beets and carrots and cauliflower. Every edible morsel that was gleaned was carefully frozen, pickled, or canned.

Mommy liked to pick cucumbers before they reached a decent pickling size. Every morning, in the dewy, wet grass, loose clippings from the reel mower plastered to her bare feet, Becky went in search of all the little cucumbers according to her grandmother's instructions. She had to lift the heavy, scratchy vines, tilt her head to the left, then to the right, and peer under the wide cucumber leaves to find every tiny pickle. Babies, that's what they were. Baby pickles with their wilting yellow blossoms still attached.

Mommy clapped her hands and chortled like a child who had won a prize when she finally had enough of these mini-cucumbers to start a batch of seven-day sweet pickles. She washed them and snipped off the ends, but then the light went out of her face. A gray shadow of doubt crept across the childlike glee, followed by a blank expression as her eyes turned dark with fear.

She had forgotten how to make seven-day sweet pickles, leaving her scrambling for a foothold, as if she needed to regain her sense of balance and had no idea where to begin. She cried softly, lifting her apron to find her wrinkled handkerchief in the deep pocket of her dress, spread across her thin legs.

Becky comforted her as best she could by showing her the recipe they would be using. But that was no use. Mommy could not grasp the concept of what cucumbers were for and had no idea what she was doing with a paring knife.

Salome mentioned the fact that a chiropractor might help; a good adjustment always did her good. So Becky cleaned up Mommy and trundled her off to the chiropractor.

And so it went. Becky learned by trial and error what worked well and what was not a good idea.

Some days she just had to wing it, the way Daniel used to say.

She thought of him more often than she cared to admit, a wistful longing that was hard to understand. Why had he asked her to be his special girl if he didn't know or care where she was now? Did he ever wonder how she was doing?

If only the administration at Round Oaks had accepted her. She would not be here, so very far from home, with only phone calls and letters to assuage the cauldron of homesickness that often threatened to boil over.

Prayers and determination, that's what it took. Each day some new and unpredictable event cropped up, and so far, with the family's input, she had done an admirable job, Mary said.

She also said they should all be ashamed. Reuben and Enos for moving so far away when they knew they had aging parents. Malinda and Anna for their quilting and letting their work stand in the way of caring for the elderly.

When Becky blurted out to Mary, "What about your market?" she was met with an indignant sputter, followed by a string of lame excuses, each one more pathetic than the last.

So there you have it, Becky thought, pushing the creaking porch swing gently with one bare foot and listening to the sound of the crickets and katydids in the garden. English people have careers, so they put their parents in the care of trained staff at an establishment built for the elderly, which the plain folks would never do.

"We care for our own," she had often heard her father say. We do. Yes, we do, Becky thought, shaking her head. But of what quality is our care? She supposed care was given in various degrees in many different families, as well as in the facilities built for the care of the aging.

She could not pass judgment, not now, not ever. She was only a young, inexperienced girl without the responsibility of her own family, so who was she to be harsh in her accounts of anyone?

Daudy and Mommy had both lost the ability to do for themselves and were dependent on her for so many things. She kept the house clean, fed them nutritional meals, and did the washing every day. Yet they were slipping, wraithlike, into a fog, except it didn't disappear into the hollows of early morning. Their days and weeks and months were leaving them weaker and more helpless. How long would she have them?

A part of her longed for home. The other part longed to stay with her aging grandparents, whom she had come to love more than she thought possible. Without a doubt, Daudy loved her. His eyes twinkled when she got out her little harmonica. He smiled his lopsided smile and told her in his blurry speech, "Play, Becky, play." And she would.

She played "Red River Valley," "Amazing Grace," "Old Dan Tucker," and many old tunes she had learned from her father. Daudy would nod his head and tap the tips of his fingers on the bedclothes, his eyes young, if only for a fleeting moment.

When she sang, the tears would roll down his craggy old cheeks and drop on his shirt front, unnoticed, as he was carried away on the wings of Becky's voice. Mommy would come bustling over, birdlike, wipe Daudy's face, shake a finger at Becky, saying "Hush, hush." She didn't understand. She was only doing what she knew.

Visitors came in the evening—family members, the ministers of the district, the group of people they had joined in worship for almost sixty-five years. When there was a knock on the door in the evening, Becky always welcomed the visitors wholeheartedly. She was glad to let them entertain her grandparents so she could slip away for a half hour for some time of quiet.

It was when the air turned crisp in the evening and the corn turned brown on the stalk, that teams of horses appeared in the fields following the binder. The men sweated in the September sun as they loaded the bundles of heavy corn. And Daudy took a turn for the worse.

The family was summoned and stood around his bed to make decisions. Becky stayed sitting with Mommy, trying to comfort her as best she could.

They wheeled him into an ambulance on a stretcher. He was taken to Lancaster General Hospital where he stabilized but never recovered. He died later that week during the night, when a cold rain began to fall and a whistling wind chased raindrops around corners, dislodging the tired leaves of fall, bending the dry, brown grasses.

It was so good to see her family when they arrived. Becky could not believe how much she had missed Nancy and her brothers. Her parents both blinked back tears as they greeted her, so glad to see their youngest daughter.

The community gathered 'round, cleaning, preparing the shop, washing walls and windows, floors and porches, raking and mowing the yard, cleaning the flower beds and garden. Food was brought in. People were assigned to manage the funeral—who would seat the congregation, who would do the cooking, and on and on. The whole place became a whirlwind of activity.

Poor Salome was so ashamed of the state of her house, but most of the women were understanding. They clucked their tongues in sympathy, saying she had had too much, far too much, with her growing family and the old parents to *fasark*. Henry was a good man, but too much was too much, they agreed.

Except for Leroy Miller sei Barbara. She grimaced when she cleaned the bathroom sink, gagged when she scrubbed the floor, pinched her mouth into a straight, hard line of disapproval, and went home and told Leroy she didn't care how depressed that Salome was, she could at least clean the commode. She'd be depressed, too, living like that. And not just that, cleanliness was next to godliness and that was no *faschtant* how those people lived. She didn't know how that fat young girl named Becky survived there, as the *daudyhaus* didn't look that way at all. She wondered if it ever had. *Hesslich dreckich.*

Leroy scratched his chin through his beard and wondered how much Jim Bates would pay him for the lame Belgian. He'd try and get him for as little as he possibly could. His wife's words fluttered around his head like annoying blackbirds, which soon went away after her voice stopped and she stuffed a bite of whoopie pie into her mouth.

It was when Becky was seated with the family, receiving visitors on the last evening of the viewing, that she saw him. His back was turned. He was so tall. But no, it couldn't be him. He would not have traveled all this way to her grandfather's viewing.

When he turned and she saw it was Daniel, knowing he had come and had remembered her, it was as
if bells began to chime somewhere in her heart. He
had come!

As he approached, she meant to keep her eyes
downcast, but when he shook her hand for a fraction
longer than was absolutely necessary, she lifted her
eyes, found the narrow blue slashes of his glad eyes,
and let her own welcome him warmly.

When he moved on down the line, greeting members of the family, Becky had to restrain the urge
to leave her chair and accompany him to view her
grandfather, gone forever from his hospital bed in
the living room. She wanted Daniel to know Daudy.
She wanted one chance to introduce him, to tell him
who this was. "A friend," she would say. "This is my
friend from Wisconsin."

Daudy's eyes would twinkle, and he would know
by the flush of Becky's face that she hoped to be his
maedle someday. Daudy knew many things he did
not speak of, Becky was sure. She mourned the loss
of this kindly old man more than she had thought
possible.

Excusing herself, she went to the bathroom and checked the mirror above the sink. She straightened her covering, swiped a few stray hairs in place, set her mouth resolutely, and went to find Daniel.

The trees were moving restlessly in the night air; a stiff breeze was coming from the north after the cold rain. A sliver of moon was reflected in a puddle, wet leaves floating on its surface. Becky shivered. Without a sweater, the night was chilling.

She found him leaning against the milk house wall, his hands in his pockets, his shoulders hunched. When he saw her approach, he stood straight, lifted his hands from his pockets, and extended them both. There were no words.

Surrounded by people all clad in black, milling about in the half-light, there was no place to talk with privacy. Daniel looked left, then right, grasped Becky's hand in his own, and started walking away from the barn.

They found a secluded spot behind the implement shed away from curious eyes. When Becky shivered, Daniel pulled her close to ward off the chill of the windy night.

"Becky, Becky."

That was all he said. They stood in silence, gladness surrounding them.

"I think of you every day, every hour."

"You do?" Becky was incredulous.

"Yeah. All the time. Why did your Dat and Mam make you do this? I can't see why they expected you to care for such an elderly couple."

His voice became genuinely distressed. "It's too much for such a young girl."

Becky laughed. "Oh, it was my own fault, for sure. You know I wanted to work at Round Oaks. I like old people. They're so wise and funny. They have lived so long and are sort of childish. They delight me, in a way."

"I don't care, it was too much."

"Seriously, yes, it was more than I bargained for. In my biggest dreams, I wasn't prepared for the homesickness, the intense longing to go back to Wisconsin."

"Why?"

"Well, my family. My home is there."

"Is that all?"

Quietly, Becky whispered, "There was you, too."

Long into the evening, they spoke of the months they had been separated, the events that had shaped their summers.

When Daniel left to spend the night at his cousin's house a few miles away, Becky was left to grapple with her own insecurity. Did he want her for his special friend, still? Or did he only care for her as a younger sister?

Would she be expected to stay on as Mommy's caregiver, or would she be expected to return with her family?

The day of the funeral was filled with October sunshine, colorful foliage, and brilliant skies the color of periwinkle flowers. A fitting day for Daudy, Becky thought, as she wept by his graveside, standing with Mommy and her parents, wearing her new black dress and black bonnet over her white covering.

She was glad to return to the homestead, her stomach growling, she was so hungry. The mashed potatoes were hot and creamy, the beef gravy thick and rich, just the way she liked it. With sliced roast beef and cheese, cold pepper slaw, and rolls with plenty of jelly and butter, Becky felt much better after she had eaten.

After the farm was cleaned up and the last of the helpers had gone home, the family gathered in Mommy's living room to make the decision. How should they care for Mommy?

First, they addressed Becky, who sat nervously pleating the hem of her apron with fast moving fingers, biting her lower lip.

Henry spoke. "What are your plans, Becky? Do you want to stay on?"

The anxiety in his voice tore at Becky's heart, knowing the life of this young farmer and his depressed wife. To leave Mommy alone in her little house was unsafe, as hazardous as pushing her across the street at midday. She would injure herself, or worse, jeopardize others' lives as well with the dementia, her inability to remember.

Becky felt torn in two. She wanted to go home, resume her carefree life, and be with Daniel, but she knew she was needed here. Then there was the big question about whether Daniel even expected her to be his girlfriend. She was barely seventeen and too young for a serious relationship, he probably thought.

She shrugged her shoulders and looked to Mam for help. Nancy spoke up, confident, commanding attention.

"She can come home with us. She's done enough. Everyone expects too much of Becky at such a young age."

Dat nodded, solemnly.

Salome raked in a hissing breath. "Well, I can't do it. My nerves won't take it."

Henry quickly patted her shoulder and said, "No, Salome, you won't have to."

Mary stuck her elbow into Anna's ribs and glowered at Salome, which was not lost on Mam.

"I'll stay," Becky said.

Salome lifted her head, hope in her dull, gray eyes.

Suddenly, little Mommy sat forward on her rocking chair, planted her feet firmly on the rug, and raised a hand. "I want to go to Wisconsin," she announced, in a clear voice.

"You can't," Reuben said forcefully.

"Why can't I?"

"Well, I don't know. You're not fit."

"What do you mean, I'm not fit? I'm fit as a fiddle. Becky is here, and she knows everything about me. All I need is a room to myself, a bed, windows to look out of, a table to read my Bible, a few chairs, and my crocheting. I want to go. I can't live here without Daudy." She began to cry in earnest, childlike little coughs and hiccups following her tears.

Becky felt her own tears rising and blinked them back quickly.

Dat looked at Mam whose face had turned pale. She sat like a stone on her chair, unable to move with the shock of Mommy's announcement.

Becky watched her mother's face and felt the battle within her. But she couldn't help thinking, "There, Mam, what you expected of your relatives is suddenly required of you. Now step up to the plate and do your share." But she said nothing.

Mam cleared her throat, knotting the Kleenex on her lap. "Well, I suppose we could give it a try."

She lifted martyred eyes to Dat, the desperation in them as plain as the nose on her face.

Dat blinked and looked to Becky for help.

Becky sat up straight, squared her shoulders, and said she could see no problem, as long as her parents were willing to make the necessary sacrifices, thinking all the while of Daniel and hoping she would soon be with him every single weekend.

"Don't they say you should never move a person away from the environment they are used to?" Mary asked.

"You mean if they have dementia?" Salome asked loudly.

Mommy perked up, small and birdlike, her eyes darting from one face to the next. "Where did you get that word? I never heard of it. Whatever you mean by it, I don't have it. Sometimes I just forget things. Everybody does."

Here she paused, her little face like a wrinkled, dried prune, and held up one thin arm, the flesh loose and soft and dotted with age spots like dark freckles, with one bony finger held aloft. "If Becky lives in Wisconsin with Enos and Sadie, then that is where I want to go."

Suddenly exhausted, she scooted herself back, laid her head on the headrest of the recliner, closed her eyes, and said nothing more.

The family discussed the good and the not so good, but in the end, Becky knew she would go home with Mommy in tow.

They made plans to haul a trailer with the things she would need. The following day they would load the trailer, clean the house, and prepare Mommy for the long trip to Wisconsin.

Becky did not sleep much that night. The joy of going home kept waking her when she dozed. The unknown about Daniel made her giddy with anticipation. Was she just too big? Too large and unattractive to him after being away for so long?

But he said he thought about her every day and he held her in his arms. But perhaps that was only because of the chill. Or perhaps he did that to lots of girls.

Ah, no. Probably not every girl would want him. He was older, twenty-two or twenty-three, she wasn't sure which, and certainly not tall, dark, and handsome. Well, that was fine with her. She wasn't either. Daniel was plenty good-looking, with his longish brown hair and narrow eyes that were blue as the sky.

He was kind and slow, a bit unconcerned, and his nose was big. But not too big.

In the late morning she hugged Salome, shook Henry's hand, and thanked them for everything they had done to help. They latched the door on the trailer, settled Mommy into the second seat of the fifteen-passenger van with two pillows at her side and a blanket across her lap. They had a bottle of water and a thermos of hot tea, a package of crackers and a small banana for her. She was as excited as a child, but as the miles fell away, she dozed, her head lolling on the plump, white pillow.

Mam seemed agitated, talking in short sentences. She was gruff to the boys and short with Dat, calming down only when the steady hum of the engine and the gentle rocking of the van lulled her into an uneasy sleep. Her chin sank into her chest, her hunched shoulders swaying with the vehicle's movement.

Becky sat in the backseat with Abner and Junior, a stab of pity for her mother and grandmother erasing the shared humor of her brothers. There she sat, hurtling along the interstate, as dependent on the driver's skill as she would surely be dependent on God to provide the skills she would need. She would be dealing with a feisty little grandmother who, far too often, did not recognize what went on around her and had become completely dependent on the orders of her caregivers—if she chose to obey.

Well, Becky thought, the wheel of life turns and takes us along, Mam. Perhaps now I will be more than just Becky, the second daughter, too large, too unpopular with the youth, and a sort of nobody, especially when Nancy's around. You'll be asking me questions about how to cope with this difficult situation.

Still, in spite of recognizing all this, Becky loved her mother with a love that was a physical ache. She knew she didn't really want to bring Mommy home to Wisconsin, but she would have felt too guilty to refuse, afraid of doing wrong by not doing her duty. Maybe this is the fear of the Lord, the principle by which we become wise. Becky shook her head with the irony of it.

To shake herself from her reverie, she punched Junior's arm, causing him to grab his forearm with the palm of his hand, squeeze his eyes shut, and howl. "Ow! Ouch! Becky, you forget how powerful you are."

"Wanna arm wrestle?" she asked.

"No."

"Why not?"

"You know why." He grinned over at Becky with his lopsided grin. She knew she could beat him at arm wrestling, every time. Well, maybe not always, but now she could.

"It's tough, isn't it, having a sister who can 'git-cha'?"

They chuckled together, Becky's infectious laugh rolling out, making Abner lean forward and turn his head to look at her. "I didn't realize how much I missed that sound, Becky."

"You missed me, didn't you? Didn't think you would, now, did you?" Becky grinned and kept smiling for miles.

CHAPTER 9

WHEN THEY ARRIVED HOME, QUICK TEARS
welled up in Becky's eyes. She flung herself through
the front door and up the steps to her bedroom where
she stood, one hand on each side of the doorframe,
drinking in the haven that was her room. It was her
own private place to be, where her furniture and pic-
tures and pillows and all her pretty things surrounded
her like friends, warming her heart with the familiar,
the safe, the loved.

Coming home was a memorable event, one she
recorded with descriptive words in her diary. Her stay
in Lancaster stamped her heart with a full and absolute appreciation of home.

They cleaned out the *sitz-schtup*, the formal living room, usually closed off by four removable doors,
or double doors, as the Amish named them. Before
church services were held in shops and garages and
basements, they were held in the house. Every piece
of furniture from the first floor was moved into the

bench wagon, the large, enclosed, horse-drawn wagon that housed the long benches used for church services, moving them to the next home that would be hosting church, or a wedding or funeral.

Now Mommy had a cozy room of her own, with the family close enough that she was not alone. The sounds of family life would be muffled, but comforting. She had no kitchen and no bathroom, but since she needed assistance with both, her new place was a good fit.

She had her beige recliner, covered with the crocheted afghan in vivid colors of red and green. On a small stand beside it, she could put her glasses, battery alarm clock, a dish of hard candy, her Bible, and, on the lower shelf, her basket of yarn containing the project of the moment. She was usually working on an afghan, using up the leftover yarn someone brought her from the Goodwill store in town.

Nearby was a small drop-leaf table with a chair pushed into each end, her single bed with a colorful nine-patch quilt, an assortment of woven rugs in brilliant colors, and a chest of drawers, with her water set on a doily. The pitcher and glasses were valuable antiques that had belonged to her grandmother. On the wall hung numerous calendars and family records, plus aerial photos, framed in oak, of the home farm in Lancaster County.

She brought her diaries along, and the family shared their copies of the weekly Amish newspaper called *Die Botschaft* and a few other periodicals like *Guideposts* and *Reader's Digest*. She seldom read now though, since she was unable to concentrate long enough to finish a story.

When it became cold and windy, the wind rising to a high whine around the eaves, the doors separating her room from the warm kitchen had to be removed, but she only allowed two to be taken away to the attic, saying she was warm enough.

She would wrap a blanket around her legs, kick up the footrest of the recliner, fold her hands in her lap, and sit, a childlike smile on her weathered face. She felt like this was her vacation, and she was enjoying her rest. No cooking or washing and no garden; only days of watching the family, listening to their talk, and resting.

This all worked well until she became bored and wanted something to do. One day she wandered out of the house while Mam was bent over the sewing machine and decided to visit the neighbors. Mam was beside herself, running to the implement shed to find Dat, her anxiety and fear rising by the second.

Of course they soon found Mommy wandering out the driveway, almost to the mailbox, talking to herself, a smile on her face, enjoying the pleasure of her own company.

When the weekend arrived, Becky was much more excited than she would have thought possible, after having been away for many months. She dressed with special care, wearing a blue dress the color of a morning sky. Her hopes were elevated to new heights, now that she had carefully relived Daniel's words over and over. She steadily pushed away specters of doubt and disbelief, twin ghosts that banished her happiness effectively. She had a chance, she told herself. That was the thing.

Ironically, they were to spend the evening singing Christmas carols at Round Oaks. A bit early, perhaps, but the administrator had asked them to come. Becky looked forward to seeing Harold Epstein, her old friend and confidant.

The evening started out well when she noticed Daniel in the backseat with his buddies, grinning at her when she climbed into the van. The squeals of welcome from the girls, and the way they paid special attention to her, were heartwarming.

It was so good to be home, so good to see the familiar houses and streets surrounding the town. She loved the feel of the clean Wisconsin air with its promise of winter and its abundance of clean, bright snow. It covered the wonderful emptiness of hills and forests and creeks like a pristine blanket, uninterrupted by traffic and skid loaders and snowplows and angry streams of people who needed to get to work and found the snow only an irritation, a setback to their ambitious day.

That one freak April snowstorm in Lancaster was all Becky had seen, but it was almost frightful, the way buggies clopped through unsafe driving conditions. Cars skidded and lost control, ending up in gardens and yards and on the backs of other vehicles. Red lights spun and sirens wailed, a spectacle that was only an added nuisance to the existing melee.

She guessed she was just a plain country girl, born and raised in boring Wisconsin, and that suited her just fine.

The singing went well, with Becky's voice blending in with the large group, adding a special bell-like quality. She loved to sing and put her heart into it, letting her voice rise and fall easily, following the words of the Christmas hymns.

She found Harold Epstein and waved, smiled, and waved again. She was rewarded with a large grin, his hand waggling in reply. As soon as she could, she made her way to him and greeted him warmly, rewarding him with her hand held in both of his as tears splashed down his lined face.

"I missed you, Becky. I missed you. It was as if all the sunshine went out of my life. I'm so glad you're back. And how are your grandparents?"

"My grandfather passed away a few weeks ago, and we brought my grandmother back to live with us."

"I'm sorry to hear it."

"Thank you. I was sad because of my grandfather's passing. He was a real friend to me, so kind and caring. I read to him every afternoon."

"You would," Harold mused. "You know you are a special girl, Becky. The young man who wins your hand will be a fortunate one."

Becky did not know how to take a compliment of such high quality. She became flustered and said something unfitting and empty. Harold laughed.

"The old Amish humility. Always humble. Always denying. That's all right, Becky. You can take it any way you want."

He paused, then his eyes took on a new light. "I have a surprise for you, Becky."

He waited, as if to heighten the drama of his announcement. "They're going to let you work here!"

Becky clapped her hands like a child on Christmas morning, her delight evident, receiving his announcement with all the joy he anticipated.

Her first day at work was two weeks before Christmas. She had had her interview with the administrator the previous week, and it went well. The only requirement was that she must wear a white bib apron, which the church allowed, just like the market workers who wore them only for their jobs.

So Becky sewed, sang, and pressed white aprons, whistling as she did so.

Mam was concerned, however. She felt as if a post of support had gone out from under her, now that Becky was gone for nine hours each day. But winter was coming on so things would not be as stressful, since Mommy would not try to venture forth. She quickly got chilly, being a little person without too much covering on her frail, old bones.

Becky promised Mam she would not go to work at Round Oaks if she needed her at home, guilt nagging her dutiful heart the way it did. But Dat would hear nothing of that, saying he was home on the farm and capable of caring for his aging mother if Mam needed a break.

Nancy spoke up, too, offering support, followed by the boys, each saying that Becky deserved to be doing what she loved best.

A great love and appreciation for her family welled up, almost spilling over and running down her cheeks in the form of tears, but her rapid blinking kept them in check. Her eyes glowed with the emotion she felt, surrounded by the light of her family's love. Only after being in Lancaster could she fully comprehend the warmth and caring she had always taken for granted.

And so a new chapter began for Becky at the age of seventeen. She learned the ropes fast. A good student, she was quick to absorb instructions from anyone who wanted to teach her. And she was always cheerful, her dry sense of humor and quick wit a spot of sunshine for many of the residents of Round Oaks.

Wherever she went around the facility, she thrived on helping the elderly. She smoothed pillows, cooled a feverish face with a fresh washcloth, read a story, changed a bed, and brought trays of food. But her most valuable talent was her listening ear and caring heart. She had a genuine interest in the cracked, whispery voices that related endless history. By the time she was there for a year, and her eighteenth birthday had arrived, she was well established as one of the best caregivers Round Oaks had been fortunate enough to hire.

Nancy had begun to date a young man named David Schmucker. She had forgotten about Allen and was headed toward marriage, quite content to have found this new person, "her meant-to-be all along," she airily confided.

Becky had given up on Daniel. She realized after a year went by that he had no romantic interest in her whatsoever, in spite of his fling with her when she was much too young to be dating seriously.

She told Nancy this one evening when they sat in Nancy's room, the bare branches of the oak trees etched against the cold light of a waning November moon. "He just runs around on the weekends and treats me like a sister, same as all the other girls, so I figure he doesn't want a fat wife. He'll likely start to date Ida Fisher soon. She's probably never seen a hundred pounds."

Nancy was examining a mole on her chin, holding a wooden mirror at a careful angle to catch the best possible light from the battery lamp. She put down the mirror, stared open-mouthed at Becky, and said, "Why would you say a thing like that?"

"Well, after a year, you know there's something wrong."

"He's nice to you."

"Same as he is to everyone."

"Do you want him? Do you act as if he has a chance?"

Becky shrugged her shoulders, lifted her chin, and said she'd never run after any guy. At her size, how embarrassing would that be, huh? And besides, she loved her job at Round Oaks, and she'd stay there till she was fifty and the size of a barrel. If Daniel wanted her, he knew where she was.

"He used to seem very interested, Becky."

"He was."

"He told you?"

"Yes."

"Perhaps he's waiting still. You're barely eighteen."

"That's old enough."

"Maybe he doesn't think so."

Suddenly shy and unable to express her feelings, Becky lifted the corner of Nancy's quilt and flung it over her head, crossed her arms, lifted one foot over the other, and sat. She sat on the floor like a statue that was covered with a tarp for repairs, making no sound.

Nancy finished examining her mole and decided to address the imperfection on the rug. She lifted the quilt and peered beneath it, finding a stone-faced Becky staring straight ahead. Grabbing the quilt, she pulled it back over her head.

"Hey! Quit acting so stupid. Get out from under that quilt."

"No, I like it in here."

"I need you to tell me how to get rid of this mole."

"You can't. Leave it there. Some people call them beauty marks."

"No they don't."

"I've heard it."

"Becky, come on. Stop acting so dumb."

As Becky got to her feet, Nancy yanked the corner of the quilt off her head. Becky grasped the opposite corner and gave a mighty tug, tearing the heavy cover from Nancy's hands. She quickly rolled herself in the quilt like a gigantic cocoon, coming to a halt in front of the dresser.

Nancy stamped her foot in frustration, then doubled over, laughing helplessly until she crumpled onto the foot of the bed and gasped for breath. Becky really did roll easily, just like a barrel or one of those blue drums that held kerosene.

Nancy heard her sister's muffled voice, then began laughing all over again. "What did you say?"

"Mm-fff-tt."

Nancy walked over and pounded a fist somewhere in the region of Becky's hip. She was rewarded by the flinging away of the quilt, a mad scramble, and a lunge in her direction. Nancy turned and fled, running down the hall and into the bathroom, slamming the door in Becky's face.

"Let me in!"

"No."

"Come on, Nancy. Let me in."

"Not if you're going to hit me."

So Nancy let her in, and they sat on the edge of the bathtub and talked. Lighthearted warmth surrounded them, that easy, comforting feeling of being with a sister you trusted, knowing she trusted you, too. You could tell her anything, and she'd be all right with whatever was on your mind, no matter how childish or fearful or silly.

"Well, Nancy, I do like Daniel. A lot. I think I almost love him, but he doesn't notice me anymore. And if I tell you this, do you promise not to laugh?"

"I promise."

"I don't know how to flirt. I mean, not flirt, but how to let someone know that I like them, or let them know in subtle ways that I would welcome them, or whatever. I mean, I have confidence in many ways, but when it comes to guys, I imagine they think I'm about as attractive as a well fed cow."

Nancy did not laugh. She merely nodded, soberly addressing this problem with kindness. "I can believe it, Becky, I can. I mean, sometimes it's hard enough when you're, you know."

"Size normal?"

"Well, yes."

"You know I'll never be thin. It's like being deported to Siberia or the North Pole if I have to try and lose weight. I can't stand to think of two grapes and a weeny cup of yogurt for breakfast."

Nancy nodded. "But I do believe Daniel cares about you, Becky."

"He said he wanted me for his girl, a long time go."

"He did?"

Becky nodded soberly.

"Well then."

"Then, what?"

"You'll have to wait, I guess. Or ask him for a date."

Becky shrieked at the humiliation of doing anything so far out of the traditional way of dating.

As Becky turned eighteen, Nancy became a true friend and support. They spent every evening in each other's rooms, talking about their jobs, boys, friends, weekends, everything. How this all came about was a bit of a mystery to Becky, but she took it, this newfound admiration of Nancy's, and loved her unabashedly. She made Nancy laugh until their sides ached, Nancy telling Becky about her insecurities that they had never discussed before. For Becky, this was liberating, freeing herself from the status of always being the runner-up, or second or third, never quite coming up to Nancy's status.

It was also a huge eye-opener. Could it be true that someone like Nancy, with her figure, face, and popularity, harbored even less confidence than she herself had? Could it really be?

Was all of this about self-acceptance? What did God think of all this vanity? He made us, she reasoned. He gave me my metabolism, my appetite, my love of food. He made me this way.

Becky was strong, healthy, and large. Nancy was not large. Or strong. Her legs hurt at night, and she constantly swallowed calcium and magnesium and Centrum gummies and gross-looking green shakes she shook up and down in Mam's Tupperware shaker till her arms dropped, as if the length and severity of her shaking would change the taste. It all tasted like spoiled silage, or worse.

So Becky threw aside the ropes of doubt that held her. She showered, dressed in the red Christmas dress Daniel loved, sprayed her hair with Nancy's "shiny stuff," polished her flat shoes, set the new white covering on her head, grabbed her coat, and was out the door when Junior had the horse ready.

She was fully expecting this Christmas gift-exchange party to be the night. The night she would try to let Daniel know that she was eighteen now, and. . . .

Well, then what would happen?

Something.

The youth all met at the home of Steve and Ada Stoltzfus, a newlywed couple who had opened their home for a night of festivities for *die youngie.*

Ada's cheeks were flushed; her husband was still in the shower. Apologetic, she said he'd soon be ready, but they could all go to the basement awhile if they wanted.

The house was lit with dozens of Christmas candles, holly branches dotted with berries, bowls of water with floating tea lights, and kerosene lamps surrounded by fresh pine. Becky was thrilled with the Christmas decorating.

Mam lit a few cheap red candles at home, but thought it too worldly to decorate so freely for Christmas. That was all right; Mam and Dat were old and conservative, and that was a safety, a harbor, a guide for her own life.

But, oh, Becky loved Christmas decorations. How thrilling would it be to do this in your own home, she thought. To have Daniel help her cut pine boughs and holly.

She would sing, and he would join in. She'd put a turkey in the oven with stuffing and baste it repeatedly with butter. Or a ham, covered in pine-apple sauce. And she would always buy soda. Diet Pepsi and Mountain Dew and sometimes root beer to make root beer floats.

She would set a pretty table with white ironstone dishes and nice cutlery from Kohl's. There would never be one green Melmac plate anywhere in her cupboards, nor would she throw mismatched silverware haphazardly alongside any scratched green plates. Neither would she ever use chipped tumblers in clear plastic like Mam bought at E&R Sales.

Mam was so content, so uninteresting, never imagining she could set a table far more attractively. For one thing, she would never, ever spend fifty dollars for a few place settings of white ironstone when she had a perfectly good set of Melmac dishes, twelve plates stacked on top of each other in her common kitchen cabinets made of birch, stained to look like solid oak. The canister set on the countertop was from Tupperware, but it was so old and sticky, it was probably the first set the company had brought out.

Mam's theory was always the same, flat and undisputable. Why get rid of something if it was perfectly serviceable and nearly as good as new? What did it matter if the years rolled by and that canister set stayed right there, holding the flour, sugar, oatmeal, and coffee the way it always had?

All these things flashed through Becky's mind as she took in the brand new belongings in Ada's kitchen. Pretty glass containers with popcorn, pasta, and tea bags. With wooden lids. Even a low basket containing different mugs in bright colors, with another glass container of coffee, one of sugar, and one containing what looked like dry coffee creamer. What a modern idea!

Becky thrilled at the prospect of having her own kitchen, her own pristine domain that she would polish and scrub, sweep and wash, singing her heart out all the while. Just the thought of hanging out thick, new towels (they would be white) made her do a little spin across the floor, only in her head.

Well, she was eighteen now. All her friends and Nancy were dating, so it was high time that Daniel stopped this waiting game. This treating her like a distant relative. Of all the nerve. He had told her he would wait for her, and here she was, dutifully caring for her grandmother, working on the farm for her father, also out of duty, and now working at Round Oaks, another dutiful job. Not that she didn't like her work, she did. More than liked. She loved it, was inspired by it.

But here, here in Ada's kitchen, a stronger inspiration hit like a full-force wind in her face, awakening a need she harbored within herself.

Was she being selfish? No. It was only normal. A normal desire to be married to someone she loved, to make a home together, a place of togetherness, two spirits melded into one life.

Because, yes, she loved Daniel. There was no one else. She loved the way he walked, the way his hair was always a bit too long over his eyebrows, his air of calm, the unhurried way he moved through his days. But most of all, his kindness. The way he never failed to stoop down and pet the dogs that greeted him, naming them something like Rover or Buster or Sam, always laughing, his small eyes crinkling at the corners.

Yes, Daniel was worth having, and it was time he stopped this nonsense.

She went about her evening with a smile on her face, but not a genuine one. It was more as if she had Scotch-taped the corners of her mouth so they would stay up.

As the evening wore on, she became increasingly nervous, her eyebrows elevated without her knowing. Slowly, her smile slipped downward and her heart dropped along with it, until she couldn't eat a bite. She just sipped on some red punch that tasted like fruit snacks but with less sugar.

Quite clearly, she did not know how to flirt. She had no idea how to go about getting Daniel's attention, now that she had come to the realization that she wanted Daniel for a husband. A real husband who lived in a house with her and cared for her until they were both as old as Mommy and Daudy had been, although, perhaps she might not live that long, being heavy and all.

Well, she didn't want to become so old that she didn't know how to make seven-day sweet pickles anymore, or until she had to live with her son, forgetting everything she was supposed to know. Finally, she could no longer take the tension of her own shortcomings and walked over to Junior, saying she was ready to go.

CHAPTER 10

JUNIOR NOISILY VOICED HIS DISAPPROVAL, TELL-ing her there was no way he was ready to leave so early. The card games were just warming up. And had she forgotten, they had not yet exchanged gifts?

Clearly embarrassed now, Becky hurried back to the girl's corner and sat down, flustered, her cheeks suffused with color. She had no interest in games. The red punch in her glass was warming by the min-ute, tasting more and more sour.

Hannah Stoltzfus irritated her by her constant shrieking as she slapped down UNO cards with the force of a hammer, always checking the room to see if anyone noticed. Her face was as red as the magenta color of her too tight dress, with her too tight apron pinned too low on her waist.

They finally exchanged gifts. Daniel sat oppo-site her, much too close and much too directly in the light of the gas lamp. She kept her eyes lowered most of the time, acknowledging Tina Lapp's effusive thanks for the glass vase and willow branches, saying she didn't have anything like it. Becky thought, no, you have everything else, her attitude turning as sour as the warm red punch in her plastic Dixie cup.

Tina was one spoiled youngest daughter. Becky had spent hours going from one expensive shop to the next, looking for a unique gift, something Tina would appreciate. Tonight, it all just irked her.

She opened her own gift, an oblong box decorated with an elaborate handmade bow, in silver. The wrapping was foil, with swirls of red, white, and silver that matched the bow perfectly. Someone surely had this gift-wrapped at the mall or some fancy store, she thought.

My goodness. A set of plush white bath towels, hand towels, and washcloths.

She opened the card carefully, a small white card emblazoned with one glittery red ornament that matched the wrapping paper. "Merry Christmas, Daniel Stoltzfus."

Becky gathered every ounce of courage she could scrape up, faced Daniel Stoltzfus squarely, and told him the towels were lovely, thanking him around the huge lump in her throat and a dozen nervous jumps in her stomach. She actually felt the color drain from her face and felt her mouth turn into sandpaper. For one wild moment she thought she might faint.

How could he have known? It was uncanny. White towels. The beginning of her dreamed-of bathroom. Had he read her thoughts?

Daniel let the warmth in his eyes radiate to Becky, the narrow shafts of blue like a possibility, the perhaps of a promise.

Becky berated her lack of confidence where Daniel was concerned, unable to understand her own inability to stand up for herself, to walk across the room and engage him in conversation the way she had always done before. Was it the newfound knowledge that she loved him? Did fear of rejection play a part?

She only knew she was miserable. The evening and all its brilliance and color had muted into a dull gray and white with black undertones. It had turned into a Christmas evening to be forgotten, or stored away in that part of her brain that kept things hidden well, a cringeworthy event that wrecked every ounce of her self-esteem.

Well, okay. If Junior wouldn't take her home, she was leaving. She had had enough. With all her usual pluck, she thanked Ada warmly and hugged her, shook Steve's hand, and without telling anyone, went to the bedroom. She dressed herself warmly in her wool overcoat, boots, gloves, and scarf, let herself out the door, and headed down the road, looking neither left nor right.

The country road was clean, the macadam cold, black, hard, and sparkling in the moonlight, the two yellow lines clearly visible. Dark pines thrust their pointed tops into the night sky like the teeth of a huge saw. The stars above winked and blinked, cold little bursts of white light, subject to King Moon. All the little stars were the citizens of its kingdom, all in their order and place.

Well, God created an awesome world, naming each star and creating every person on Earth according to His will. So it was up to Him to move Daniel. She didn't have the power.

In all things other than Daniel, I do have plenty of spunk. Confrontation with the Salomes and Nancys and Mommys of this world—no problem. I can

talk freely to older people, make friends for life with
Harold Epstein, even tell the Round Oaks administrator a thing or two, which had obviously not been
appreciated.

She was a failure now, though, because of Daniel.

The night air was crisp and cold, so cold, in fact,
that it hurt her throat, probably from all that awful
red punch, she thought.

She figured she had about three and a half miles
to go, but that was all right. No one was on these
country roads after midnight anyway. If they were,
it would be rather scary though. What if a carload of
unsavory characters came barrelling over the next rise
and decided to make off with her? They'd have a hard
time dragging her off, that was sure. She could arm
wrestle Jake and Junior down pretty easily, so there
you were.

She shivered, pulling her scarf closer. She passed
two houses set in the middle of a hill, without trees
or shrubs to break up the square structures set on
the white expanse. Like hotels on a Monopoly board.
Not even porches. She had never noticed those two

houses before. Well, in the dark, everything was changed, even the silhouettes of everyday houses.

She had almost passed them when a dark blur to her left caught her attention. She was barely aware of any sound at all, only the whisper of padded feet on snow and the realization that there was now a dark shape following her soundlessly. She gathered all her senses and became alive, calculating, taking stock of her situation.

Dogs that bark and wag their tails are not dangerous.

Dogs that bark and show their teeth are dangerous.

Dogs that do not bark but slink after you are dangerous.

Never look a dog in the eye. Keep walking. Don't panic. If you are afraid, they can smell it and they will bite you.

She turned her head slightly. He wasn't there. Good. He left. Lost interest.

She turned her head to the other side. Oops. Oh, my word. He's right behind me.

The backs of her legs tingled, waiting for the chomp that was sure to come. She could feel the sharp canine teeth break the skin above her boots.

She increased her stride, her breath coming in quick puffs.

He was still there, still walking without sound to her right.

Reasonably, Becky figured, if this deadly stalk continued for any length of time, the fact that she would be bitten by this dog would be secondary to her demise caused by a heart attack. How could one dependable organ suddenly go so haywire?

Either way, dog bite or heart attack ("Coronary"? No, "cardiac arrest," is what Harold called it), one was bound to happen, so she may as well behave like a grown-up. Face the situation head-on. It had to be easier than facing Daniel next to that propane gas light that was brighter than the sun.

Becky stopped, fully expecting the piercing of her leg by the evil, shadowy dog slinking behind her. Slowly she turned.

She stood still, watching in disbelief as she saw the dark figure of a little dog, back arched and ready to flee. She glimpsed its face, with its hurried, despairing look, and its matted tail, tucked between two back legs.

"Dog!" Becky said. She hadn't planned to talk to the dog. But she didn't know what else to do, now that the dog cowered before her, far more afraid of her than she had been of it.

Becky clapped her hands to chase it away, but she was rewarded with the steady thumping of a tail. A high whine sounded from the region of the dog's head, although it was hard to tell exactly where the sound was coming from, the way its head was lowered and turned back.

Becky drew closer, then reached out a hand. The tail began wagging furiously. In the pale light of the moon, with the snow's sparkle reflecting the light, she could see that the dog was thin and shivering, its fur matted, wet, and dirty.

Becky watched the dog, then looked again at the houses etched against the night sky like two dark ghosts. She thought of the Christmas package she was carrying with the thick, white towels. Overwhelming pity for the cold, starving creature started like a cat's purring and rose steadily within her until she dropped to her knees and reached out to the freezing and frightened dog.

She tore at the Christmas package, grabbed a towel, and swaddled the little dog, wrapping it closely while it wriggled furiously, repeatedly trying to lick her face, whining and yelping with happiness all the while.

She'd take the dog up to the houses, ring doorbells or knock or whatever, and find out who its owners happened to be. It was quite a climb up the hillside on packed snow, carrying the bundle that now lay still while clutching the remainder of her Christmas package.

At the first house, the shadows created by the silver moonlight gave her the creeps. What if a large dog burst out of the door or the owners became irate? She was wakening them in the middle of the night.

She rang the bell, putting the tip of her index finger on the oblong glow of orange light and listening to the pealing sound somewhere in the depth of the square house. She waited, holding the dog, who lay surprisingly still for all the wriggling it had done before.

There were sounds of shuffling feet, and then a voice called out, anxious, thin, and crackly.

"Did you lose a dog?" Becky asked hopefully.

The door was flung open by the biggest woman Becky had ever seen. She was all of six feet tall with an enormous girth, the belt of her bathrobe hanging loose like an untied shoe. Her hair was done up in a silk kerchief, and she was as dark as the door behind her. She began to praise the Lord immediately, lifting her large face to the sky and thanking God with all the strength and power of her stalwart frame.

She reached for the dog, crooning, "Tinker, Tinker, Tinker." Holding it to her face, she kissed it repeatedly, then moved across the foyer to call up the stairs in a tone of voice that sounded like a bugling elk. High and fierce.

They were soon joined by another massive human being who lumbered carefully down the steps, rubbing his eyes with the backs of his hands, blinking, and commanding his wife to calm down with the yelling. When she thrust the small bundle into his arms, she was rewarded by a loud burst of praise and thanksgiving, followed by a raucous snort as tears glistened on their way down his dark, well rounded cheeks.

"My baby. My baby!" he chanted over and over as the thin little dog wriggled and lapped at his face.

Becky stood in the cold on the stone doorstep, unsure of what to do next as the couple lost themselves in more loud words of praise, sobbing and crying, laughing, and passing the dog from one to the other. The new white towel was no longer white where it had covered the dog.

By and by they asked Becky to come in, have tea, and warm herself. They pressed a thick roll of bills into her hand, then launched effusive thanks all over again.

"You have no idea, honey, no idea, how we've suffered. She's our baby. She was gone for almost a week," the lady said, becoming quite breathless between sips of her tea. Her husband was heating ham bits and broth as he dried the little dog with his own towel. He had handed the new dirty one to Becky as if it was the robe of a king.

Becky was finally on her way about an hour later, the roll of bills in her coat pocket a comforting bulge and reward for all she'd been through. She smiled to herself about these very large people with the little dog they obviously loved as if it were a child.

What Becky did not know was the frantic activity at Steve's and Ada's house when Junior discovered that she was nowhere to be found.

No one had seen her leave. Yes, her coat was missing, her boots and her Christmas package. Everyone thought about it. She had not been her usual self, but why would she disappear? Junior felt especially responsible, having refused to take her home when she was ready.

Steve and Ada had retired for the night, but after a while someone wakened them, desperate to see what they might know. Oh, yes, she'd told them good-bye. She was walking home, she said.

"Walking?" Junior shouted.

"What is wrong with her?" Jake echoed. "She knows it's not safe."

General chaos followed as the boys dressed in their winter clothes and went out to get cold, restless horses hitched to creaking, frozen buggies. Becky was suddenly on everyone's mind.

Daniel's face was like stone. He showed no emotion and said nothing. His eyes were cold and calculating as he measured the distance in his mind, the hour at which she'd left, the hills, the deep pine forests, the stretches of road that were lined with houses where she'd be safe, if something had happened.

No, it was not safe for one lone girl to walk a dark country road by herself. He knew Becky was strong, but she was not strong enough to thwart an assailant, especially if there was more than one. Heartsick, his fingers trembled against the cold snaps of the britchment. He wanted to blame someone, anyone. He felt like strangling Junior. Why hadn't he taken her when she asked?

The image of Becky's unusually sad face stayed with him as he turned his horse, who reared, snorted, and then plunged into the night, scattering hard bits of snow and gravel as his hooves dug into the frozen ground.

Becky was visiting with her newfound friends, oblivious to the fact that she had caused quite an uproar.

They did not find her at home, which brought on near panic. Dat and Mam were brought stumbling from their beds in disbelief. Dat calmed everyone by saying one team should drive back to Steve's and Ada's house and make sure she hadn't changed her mind and stayed, perhaps falling asleep somewhere, if she hadn't been herself. Mam said she had been coughing and sniffling around that day.

Without a word again, Daniel charged out the drive and down the road, the buggy swerving dangerously as he goaded his horse, his heart like the weight of a cement block near the region of his stomach. Waves of nausea and fear overcame him. He had never prayed out loud the way some folks did, but he did now. He begged God to help him, to help Becky.

"You know I've been waiting till she's old enough. You know how hard it's been, how great the sacrifice. Why would this happen now?"

Over and over, he berated himself for lost opportunities, for time he now felt had been wasted.

He saw the dark figure at a mailbox, but being so distraught he didn't believe it was Becky at first. When he saw the torn Christmas package, he stifled the sob in his throat, knowing that men, real men, don't cry about one girl who has lost her way.

Becky stood waiting for the fast moving team to pass her so she could continue on home. But the horse was suddenly pulled to a stop, rather violently she thought, the door was pushed back, and Daniel jumped to the ground, very tall and very upset, loudly asking her what she thought she was doing, traipsing around the dark countryside at this hour, knowing full well it was completely unsafe for a young woman to do something so foolish. Why didn't she tell them she was leaving? Where had she been when all those teams were charging down the road, and none of them getting as much as a glimpse of her?

Daniel stamped his feet and swung his head, jerked on the reins and called, "Whoa!" about every thirty seconds when his horse wanted to run.

Becky's eyes became wide with disbelief, then wonder. This was Daniel, the calm, the unperturbed, always in control, always kind one. Yet here he was, yelling at her like she was a first-grader caught stealing candy, making her feel positively furious.

"Stop yelling at me!" she shouted.

"I'll yell if I want to. You should be spanked. Get in the buggy!" Daniel shouted right back.

"No! I'll walk."

"Get in."

"What do you care if I walk home?"

Daniel lifted his face to the sky in frustration, knowing too late that this was going all wrong. Lowering his voice, he said more kindly, his words scalloped with anxiety, "Your parents are waiting to hear from me before they call the police."

Becky's mouth fell open. She squeaked only a bit, like a mouse, before she climbed into the buggy and sat, her hands folded around the ruined Christmas package and the white towel.

The steel wheels scraped against the iron roller as Daniel made a sharp turn. Her head flew back as the horse lunged against the collar, taking off in the opposite direction as horses will do when it's cold and they are tired and want to get home to their cozy box stall with a fresh block of good timothy hay.

Total silence in the buggy. Only once did Becky have the nerve to turn her eyes sideways, finding Daniel's profile formidable. Mount Rush-more. Etched in stone. Whoo.

She was amazed at the number of buggies parked in the lane. Every light in the house was burning, turning the dark windows into rectangles of yellow, welcoming light. Thankfully, there were no police cars.

Becky was embarrassed, but assured them all that she was fine—and would likely have remained fine without all the hullabaloo. She must have been visiting with the Joneses she said, telling the group about the little dog named Tinker. She thought everyone was making an unnecessary fuss, for sure.

Mam shivered, looked positively mortified by her brash approach to finding the dog's owner. She told Becky a bit coldly to get to her bed. It was late and she needed her sleep. Mommy would be awake early, banging around, wanting her tea and *toast-brod*.

Becky almost said, "Well now, ain't that some-pin'?" But she didn't. Only your mother could irk you in that special way, making you feel like noth-ing but trouble. Someday she would write a book of "Mother-isms," a whole list of things mothers say without thinking of the consequences.

A hand at her elbow made her turn to find Daniel. "Come with me, Becky. For a buggy ride."

The last thing on her mind just then was Daniel and being married to him. Or her complete puzzlement about how to have a relationship with him. So she blurted, "Why?"

"I want to talk to you."

"What about?"

"Becky."

"You heard my mother. Time for me to go to bed."

"Please. Come with me for a buggy ride."

So Becky went, minus the heart palpitations, the worry, the longing. She felt nothing at all.

The horse must have resigned himself to steady traveling after the excitement of the previous hour, leaving Daniel relaxed. One hand expertly manipulated the reins, while the one nearest Becky found her hand and held it lightly.

"Becky, the reason I became so upset is probably evident, right?"

"I never knew you could become quite so rattled. Why?"

"Well, I was afraid something had happened to you. I can't deal with a future without you in it."

At first, his words had a dreamlike quality, as if they came from a distance. "I'm not real good with words, so I'll just tell you that I'm still waiting."

Becky took a deep breath. "Waiting for what?"

"Waiting until you're old enough to start dating an old scruff like me."

"What does age have to do with it?"

"Nothing, if you don't think so. But I'm old."

There was silence bursting with promise as Becky looked out of the buggy window. They were passing the deep black forest of pine, bathed in the light of the cold winter moon, the road stretching ahead of them like a yellow-striped, dark ribbon.

Wasn't life unbelievable? How desperately she had tried on her own, worrying herself sick about her own abilities, or lack of them, trying to figure out a job that would be the right fit. Then there's been Daniel and his inscrutable behavior. First, she cared for two grandparents, relieving the family and doing something she loved. And now, when she had let go and stopped scheming about snaring Daniel in the future, here she was, plopped into his buggy, she guessed by the giant hand of God, smack where she wanted to be.

"Becky, I want you. I want you for my girlfriend. I want to have every weekend filled with your presence, until some happy day, if God wants us together, you'll be with me every day and night, never to be away from me again. I have waited long enough."

Daniel sighed. "Tonight when I thought you were lost, or that something bad may have happened, I can't find words to express how I felt."

Becky looked at Daniel, finding his face sincere and soft with emotion. "But if you care so much, Daniel, why did you ignore me for a whole year? You acted as if I didn't exist."

For a long moment, there was only the sound of steel wheels on macadam, coupled with the steady clopping of the horse, that dull thunking rhythm that is both restful and peaceful. This well trained horse dutifully drew a carriage through the cold winter night, its occupants wrapped warmly in a plaid buggy blanket as stars twinkled in the dark night sky like bits of diamond.

Finally, Daniel spoke. "I was going to ask you when I went to Lancaster for your grandfather's funeral. In fact, that is why I went. But—and you're going to laugh about this—there are so many more presentable young guys in Lancaster than me. And you're so perfect, Becky, so soft and adorable. You're just a beautiful young girl who I figured every one of them would want."

Becky gasped audibly. "Not one of them even looked at me. Daniel, seriously, you must know that I'm larger than most girls. I'm fat. That's a real turn-off for lots of men."

Daniel spoke forcefully. "You are not fat. You're just right. If you were thin you wouldn't be you, my sweet Becky."

And with that declaration, he released her hand, slid his arm along the back of the seat, and drew her close to his heart, where he wanted her always. And when he bent his head, he only kissed her forehead quickly, like a child, a seal of endearment, a gift of his love. He was driving, after all.

But when Becky raised her face and kissed him thoroughly, a whole year of longing unspoken, he thought a star had fallen straight through the roof of the buggy, lit with a blinding light.

"So there, Daniel Stoltzfus. You've ignored me long enough."

Daniel had no words. He was completely flummoxed.

"And, if you're being truthful, then I suppose I was made for you and you were made for me. God knows what he's doing. His presence will always remind me how fortunate I am to have you." Becky spoke softly, with reverence.

"We are blessed to have each other," Daniel replied.

And as the horse clopped on through the winter night, Becky thought those white towels had been a good omen. The Christmas gift he had purchased was the perfect fit for the bathroom she had planned.

She sighed happily. Becky Stoltzfus. Mrs. Daniel Stoltzfus.

Glossary

Calf starter—nutritional pellets fed to young calves

Chvistats—relatives

Da Enos sei schveshta Mary—Enos' sister Mary

Daudy—Grandpa

Daudyhaus—a small addition to a farmhouse, built as living quarters for grandparents

Denke—thank you

Die Botschaft—name of an Amish newspaper, meaning "message"

Die youngie—the young single people, usually between sixteen and twenty-one years of age

Dya fasaufet ihn noch—You will drown him yet

English—someone whose first language is English

Enos sei Sadie—Enos' wife Sadie

Enosa—both Enos and his wife, Sadie

Errforing—experience

Fasark—to look after, take care of

Faschtant—to make sense

Fett maedle—overweight girl

Freundschaft—extended family

Green Pastures—a mental health facility

Grosfeelich—cocky, sure of oneself

Gute arpsa—good peas

Hesslich—very much

Hesslich dreckich—very dirty

His maedle—girlfriend

Kaltgraut—cole slaw

Kesslehaus—part of the house which Amish
    families use as a catch-all place for coats, boots,
    umbrellas, laundry, and even for tasks such as

mixing calf starter, warming baby chicks, and canning garden vegetables

Macht's gute!—very good!

Miede Binnichs—name of the children's prayer that begins, "Now I lay me down to sleep . . ."

Mitt die zeit—in time

Mol viddda eich sayna—to see you once again

Mommy—Grandma

Mommy, du bisht net fit—Grandma, you are not fit to do this.

Ons' Daudy Esha—at Daudy Eshes'

Phone shanty—Most Old Order Amish do not have telephone landlines in their homes so that incoming calls do not overtake their lives, and so that they are not physically connected to the larger world. Many build a small, fully enclosed structure, much like a commercial telephone booth, somewhere outside their house where they can initiate phone calls and retrieve phone messages. (Amish men with businesses may use cell phones on a restricted basis.)

Roasht—chicken filling or dressing

Rumschpringa—"running around." The time in an Amish person's life between age sixteen and marriage. Includes structured social activities for groups, as well as dating. Activities usually take place on the weekend.

S' Dat's sinn net goot—My parents are not doing well.

Scrapple—trimmings of pork mixed with cornmeal, then shaped into loaves that can be sliced and fried. Usually eaten for breakfast.

S' Daudys—grandparents

S' Grishtag essa—the big Christmas dinner

Siss net chide—it isn't decent, normal, or right

Sitz-schtup—the living room, used only for visiting with special guests

Stewed crackers—saltines (or other snack crackers) soaked in hot milk, then drizzled with brown butter. Sometimes eaten for breakfast, for a quick lunch or supper, or as a snack.

Toast-brod—toast bread

Uf da hof—in the same yard

Unedich gelt chpent—unnecessary money spent

Vett Millich—want milk

Vocational class or school—attended by fourteen-year-old Amish children who have completed eight grades of school. These students go to school three hours a week and keep a journal—which their teacher reviews—about their time at home learning farming and homemaking skills from their parents.

Other Books by
Linda Byler

*Available from your favorite bookstore
or online retailer.*

"Author Linda Byler is Amish, which sets this book apart both in the rich details of Amish life and in the lack of melodrama over disappointments and tragedies. Byler's writing will leave readers eager for the next book in the series."
–Publisher's Weekly review of *Wild Horses*

LIZZIE SEARCHES FOR LOVE SERIES

BOOK ONE   BOOK TWO   BOOK THREE   TRILOGY   COOKBOOK

SADIE'S MONTANA SERIES

BOOK ONE   BOOK TWO   BOOK THREE   TRILOGY

LANCASTER BURNING SERIES

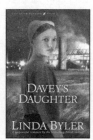

BOOK ONE   BOOK TWO   BOOK THREE   TRILOGY

HESTER'S HUNT FOR HOME SERIES

BOOK ONE   BOOK TWO   BOOK THREE

THE LITTLE AMISH
MATCHMAKER
A Christmas Romance

THE CHRISTMAS
VISITOR
An Amish Romance

MARY'S CHRISTMAS
GOODBYE
An Amish Romance

BECKY MEETS HER
MATCH
*An Amish Christmas
Romance*

About the Author

Linda Byler was raised in an Amish family and is an active member of the Amish church today. Growing up, Linda loved to read and write. In fact, she still does. Linda is well-known within the Amish community as a columnist for a weekly Amish newspaper.

Linda is the author of four series of novels, all set among the Amish communities of North America: Hester's Hunt for Home, Lizzie Searches for Love, Sadie's Montana (whose individual titles are *Wild Horses*, *Keeping Secrets*, and *The Disappearances*), and the Lancaster Burning series.

Linda has also written three Christmas romances set among the Amish: *Mary's Christmas Goodbye*, *The Christmas Visitor*, and *The Little Amish Matchmaker*.

Linda has co-authored *Lizzie's Amish Cookbook: Favorite recipes from three generations of Amish cooks!*